THE MARINER'S STAR

Also by Candida Clark

The Last Look
The Constant Eye

The Mariner's Star

Candida Clark

review

First published in 2002
by REVIEW

An imprint of Headline Book Publishing

10 9 8 7 6 5 4 3 2 1

Cataloguing in Publication Data is available from the British Library

ISBN 0 7553 0100 5

Typeset in Perpetua by Avon Dataset Ltd, Bidford-on-Avon, Warks

Printed and bound in Great Britain by
Clays Ltd, St Ives plc

HEADLINE BOOK PUBLISHING
A division of Hodder Headline
338 Euston Road
London NW1 3BH

www.reviewbooks.co.uk
www.hodderheadline.com

To Dominic, with love – for everything.

Incipit vita nova Dante

Acknowledgements

[illegible] thanks and gratitude [illegible]
[illegible]

Acknowledgements

With immense thanks and gratitude to Jonny Geller and Charlotte Mendelson.

1

It is just past dawn by the time I set out to sea, with a soft south-westerly blowing warmish in the half-light, and the first slim rays of sunshine sliding stealthy from the east. The tide is steady and high, not yet turning but holding the boat sure and fine as I slip through the harbour on a carrying swell, the great worn heaves of motion flowing shorewards from the black North Sea.

All the other boats are still at anchor, and when I'm gone, the harbour is a perfect glass again, reflecting sky. There are no sounds from off the land, no cars or human voices. Even the gulls are silent, with only the rush of engined water to tell me I'm unsleeping. But my heart is racing an unnatural pound of trouble in my chest, and if this were dreams, I say to myself, then surely I'd not be aware of that dark fear, as though every inch of forwards motion invites a harm that nothing on this earth might salve.

So I have my shoulders squared in readiness for I know not what, my feet set firm against the hull. I could be setting out in perfect innocence, I tell myself, with nothing in me but the thought of fish. But there is no respite in that lie, and no pretence left I can turn to and find help. Ahead there's nothing but the sea, a discovering roll of power that's inconceivable, spun on and out of view. It catches me the second I'm beyond the gullet of the cliff-bound harbour. I feel it snag against the tiller, goading me to turn the boat about, though I'll not budge from off this course, not now.

I'd decided, before, that I wouldn't even look back, that I'd face the sea with the land behind me and spare it no thought. But I can't do it. There's no chance of it, and it's like my neck's on a spring, wired back to the vanishing shore.

And so here I am, skewed right round and angling for remorse but finding none, not one slip of regret to catch me out and make me falter. There's only this haloed vision of infinite remoteness: the place I've spent my whole life attached to, my feet plumb down into the earth as though it were the only place I belonged, and yet the whole thing now diminished to a painted backdrop of unimportance. Because it never belonged to me, nor I to it. I only ever belonged to him. He was my homeland, the soil I grew up in, the ocean I swam in. And it's as though this plain fact is a loaf of risen bread just handed out the sky – fantastic-seeming, like something read about yet never tasted.

I shift back round to face the sea, and by now I'm almost smiling. Because what need have I of land, when he's no longer on it? None whatsoever. So I'm putting the solid banking green and grey, the massed, obsidian nest of granite houses chuffing smoke – I'm putting the whole damn thing at my back, like it's a magnet that'll only work if I'm fool enough to look at it.

But still there's the scent of brackish stream-water and earth, of early wood smoke and singeing late summer clifftop meadow grass – all this still there, and God help me I must be a lump of stone not to look back at it all once more, my jaw starting to ache with being clenched so hard against this near temptation, everything that's most familiar flooding out behind me though not dissolving, in fact lurking there like a rope leading only to a strong hemp noose, primed and fatal.

I bend my ears to the rumbled hush of the ocean, shutting them as best I can to the memory of footsteps on cobble, the endless baby-wail of gulls and the lisping fact of a land-locked breeze amongst hay, all these things that until this morning fitted so snug around my grief I'd thought they'd almost save me. But they have not. The earth has failed me. There's not been enough to keep me fixed to it because what would I be then? No better than an idiot tree, aiming skywards for no reason beyond the dumb continuance of life that meant not a thing to me, not any longer.

Beneath the keel the sea runs swift and curious as I head towards the open water. But still the land is there, dazzling as a neckchain locked about my throat so I can't unclasp it, however much I wrestle and strain. No, that's not the way, I tell myself, seeing my life like a string of beads I must meditate on in order to forget.

So I try to fix all these land-memories in my mind and hold them steady there, and delicate, as though by pushing them through the sieve of rational thought I can diminish them and that way forget them, because anyway – and here I feign a courage that I do not feel – what must possess me now is this: to get away out to sea to find him. That's my life now. And I must do it. I'll just not be true to myself otherwise.

2

When I take a peek over the edge there's nothing left of the earth beneath, only an inky thickness of fat and glistening blue. Already there's no guessing at its depth. Each motion forwards means the sea grows darker, and yet where the wind touches it the darkness shudders, trembling.

I pass beyond the harbour buoys, steering a course within the channel of deep water. Some way ahead I can see the flags that mark the place the lobster pots are set, though beyond that there's nothing but the sea. The line of the horizon is barely drawn. It shimmers nacreous as a heat haze, evaporated by proximity.

Still there's no tide to pull or push me either way

but there's a swollen sense about the sea, as though it's readying itself for fights, stirring deeply far beneath – the sea bed in fact a monster's back, wrinkling with thoughts of trouble. Small waves gather close about the boat, hurrying it forwards, breaking in quick folds about the prow so that the air grows damp with spray.

I'm drawn clear out of sight of the harbour now, and the cliff side looms massive, vaster than an ocean liner. Even though I've crept along its base throughout my life, from on the water it seems grander than I'd ever have thought possible. It burns on fire from top to bottom with early flames of dawn, the light pressed full against it.

Sliced clean crossways, the earth is readable and revealing, built in layers of ochre and fox-red russet, crammed with hidden seams of crystallite and jet. Degrees of peaty darkness fade into the pale of sandstone embellished with a thousand gull-dropped paintings. And as I move further from the land I can see the tufted green of clifftop meadows, virulent against the thrush-egg sky, faint as cornflowers bleached by sun.

There's the boom of profound water crashing heavy against the hidden reef, and the sound is sudden in my ears as I come round into the lee of the buttressed cliffs, wondering how far beneath the surface danger lies. When the tide is down, how many times I've walked the miles round the headland to the next village, gathering up the dancing crabs that're caught in pools when the water's ebbed to leave them stranded, stuffing the snapping things in a bag, mindful they don't peck me as I push them there. Dark often makes them docile, so it's safe enough.

But no more of that life now, I tell myself, wishing that the fact my eyes are averted was enough to stop me thinking of the land. It's because there's still the smell and the sound of it, that's the reason. Yet even now the sound is diminishing. I can hear only the last part of its echo from the secret caves where the sea boils along the bottom of the cliff as though to topple it, or gnaw at its foundation till it crumbles.

And I know the sea will do it. It's happening right along this north-eastern coast, the entire line of it already become raggedy and broken like a brittle spine made powdery with pounding. But it's a delicate erosion and all the drama of it is seasonal. In summertime, you'd not think the sea was capable of the rage it has in winter. Then, it is unsafe even to go near the thing, which comes up higher, or so it seems, with every passing year, smashing up the houses on the shoreline and hurling bricks and rocks through windows, shattering its way indoors.

So will it be that one day the cliffs are scoured right down and rubbed away to nothing more than beaches, broken up and worn by all the heaps of years, like someone's taken a file to them? For sure that's how it'll be, and there'll be no triumph then of either sea or land but just a pointless mashing of the two – just a namelessness, forgetting.

I keep my eyes fixed seawards, trying not to think on the coffin-stacked past that's brought me and everyone like me to this point, wondering about the land's fast tip towards the sea. Because how soon will it be? It must be fairly soon, I'm sure of that much, and though I'll not see it, someone's children will.

3

It's a Sunday, and all the other boats are idle. I remember standing beside the kitchen calendar with a pencil (I'd not had the nerve then for a pen), and circling today's date. One year, I'll wait for one year to the day.

I imagined the pointless revolutions on the clock face, the sloughed off scraps of calendar days without content, and I knew that one year or ten, time would mean nothing but waiting. But the fact that the date fell on a Sunday had made the whole thing possible: it would not do to be flocked by men from the village, bobbing about me with nags and reprimands. For sure they would have asked questions. *Now then, is that you? And what're you thinking of, setting out in your husband's boat like you've got a right to? Turn back, do you hear?*

No, they would not have allowed it. Well, they're allowing it now, I think to myself, because they've no notion of what I'm up to, and no way on earth of preventing it. I've left, fair and square, and there's nothing any living soul can do about it.

I think of the men then like lemmings all snug beneath scratchless blankets, the village at peace in a dogged harmony of rest, while beneath them in their houses there'll be wives forever fretful, clasping at the sounds their husbands make in the bad-sprung bed above their heads, snatching at them with such greed because they could be the last sounds of them they'll ever hear, and how they hate the men for making this be true. So it goes, and I do know what I'm speaking of, by God I do.

And when the men at last rise, they'll hive off down the pub without much word, spitting, most likely, and their wives will knit their thoughts to some kind of woolly order that covers their heart like a poorly made rug, a thing with holes in it just like the nets they'll be mending, too, which let all the fishes they could live on run back fast and agile to the sea.

It's regulations that says it should be so. But is it regulations that say there's no recompense either for the hearts of those that are left behind? There's no regulation of any kind then, whichever way you try to dress it. There's only the soul unbound in grieving, in a pattern that'll outlive us all. This is entirely true, as though it were written down somewhere that it should be so.

From this short way distant now I cannot help but turn again to see the entire village, snug and restful there within the rosy arms of cliffs. Inches above the water's skin there's a soft mist risen and unmoving. It seems to hover, too, across the shortened stretch of beach and run seamless right up over the rooftops like sleep. No fires have yet been lit and I can see no figure there awake – there's no sign of smoke or light or motion, just the unbroken seal of faded night. I can almost hear the hard machinery of breath and waiting, the minds still scribbling out secret stories. The houses seem anything but empty.

The sun is really rising now, steady and tremendous, and if they're quick about it, it'll be fine weather for the harvest back on land. I can see the risen dust from shattered corn heads, the fields right along the coastline transformed in days to something foreign-seeming and emphatic, the silent cylinders of straw like beacons along the cliffs. Some places have made a start on the harvest already. I can sniff it from right out here, something hay-feverous upon the air that attracts the light, making it seem evanescent, swarming with luminosity like a thousand ghostly bees, the atmosphere humming and sweet.

But there's no warmth yet from the sun and my face is braced against the morning motion of sea-air on skin, an unkind thing, even though I'm not yet out in the open water, with the boat still chugging in the lee of the cliff head. For how many years have I watched the boats leave and vanish? All my life I have done this – like all the mothers before me, knowing I'd not depart the fate set out for me but would stay, and endure it.

And yet now it's me that's leaving and vanishing – I frame this thought like a magic trick, not yet believing that it's true. Because I have never before set foot in this boat, never set sail upon the sea before this day. It is bad luck, or so they say, for a woman to go aboard her husband's fishing coble.

4

And for a second I see myself as I must look from on shore – a solitary figure in a small boat, departing. So in my mind's eye it's me who's back on land, watching as I have watched a thousand times the diminishing signal of all certainty, fading to darkness. I can see myself quite clearly there, just as I was on that last day, a woman of late middle-age, ordinary, forgettable, lit with gladness only at the sight of him, my best beloved, and I see myself there, back on shore, with what gleam there was about me fast clouding over until there's nothing left but a kind of grey hopelessness as I watch him disappear into the sea. And it's only when he is quite out of sight that I turn back to face the land and bury myself once more inside the nest of streets.

But hidden as I am, it makes no difference: all the seconds that he's gone I have him in my skin like a wish, nervous for his return. I can hear the water-splash of his boat setting out, the slither of painter over iron as he casts off, the gasping engine insubstantial and breathless-seeming in the face of the sea. And I watch him slipping away to find the horizon, digging up fish on his ploughed return, furrowing across the water for home.

First, though, there'd always be this: his back turned, his left hand raised in farewell, his right upon the tiller, his eyes fixed seawards like he was finding his way down a slender tunnel I couldn't possibly fit. And would I hate him then? Would I hate him for the way he left me shorebound and without him? No, it was not hatred, though it might have been hatred's cousin, since in my veins it felt almost like it, as though I'd been taken over by some kind of broiling, rolling heat of fear that I couldn't get clear of, however much I dodged it. It would rest there in me for all the moments of his absence, some kind of childish anguish that stamped its foot against my guts telling me it wasn't right for him to be leaving me like that, setting his back to me in a way that told me he was smiling – choosing the sea over me.

And it was true. Even in his sleep he longed for the ocean. He would wake me with trembles before dawn, his body forgetting its sea legs in the brazen honesty of night, leaving only the fear, which drew him to it with mermaid clutches I could never compete with. I'd watch his eyes' fast flickerings, and I'd wonder where his gaze was resting. Not on me, I was sure of that much, but pinned far out among the softly stacking waves, concealing fish and unglimpsed treasure that tormented him, sending him back there each day with an expression half mad with desire, his body tight-strung like a bow he'd learnt to hold taut and braced against the nuzzling sea.

I'd scoop his big frame up in my arms then, the flesh silken and pliant where the wind and sea had not got to it, and where it had the grooves and ridges of skin puckered up with salt-whipped days spent plumb in the thick of it, the world seizing him – that's how he described it to me once – seizing him and doing what it would with him whether he liked it or no. And his Viking's hair would be against my face as I held him, his chin-bristles pressed against my throat, nestled in the crook of it like a rare thing in a box, and I'd be sure of his breath, the fact of the life within him, as it whispered and sighed into the empty space all around me, the space that soon he would make real by going.

Sometimes, when there were storms and the boats couldn't set out, he would wake up cursing, his brow shadowed with worry at bills unpaid and debts dishonoured. I would have to turn away from him then, for fear he'd catch me smiling. I'd not be able to help myself, never being anything but glad when he couldn't go out, even though on days like that he'd be away from me for longer, often, and be messing about with oil-soaked rags upon his boat, at anchor in the tide-drawn beck.

So I'd hold him steady and close against me through the wind-wracked nights, feeling his nearness like an answered prayer I'd soon have to pay for with some act of penance not yet exacted, but imminent and certain. And I'd stay like that, one eye on the first signs of weather from around the curtain edges – I learnt to tell the weather that way, just by the variations in early light, divining rain from limpid curlicues of unleavened dawn creeping into the room from behind cloth, just small signs of moonshine-looking light which would be enough to tell the ocean's sentiments.

And it was as though those curtains were a veil over my entire future: would the weather be faithful or false? I would wonder which way the fates would have it, and would long to rip down that veil and see into the bloodied true heart of things to discover what lay there – hell or happiness. I was hostage to that weather-vane window, and would be restless most nights until those first thoughts of morning, which I hated: by then the die was cast.

This morning was no different, except I was alone. I lay bolted to the rack of that bed and watched the fading night, the stars diminishing, and then the moon's last glow extinguished by the hidden sun, a weight of fire smouldering, undoused, beneath the waterlogged horizon. And as I lay there, the sea's hush a thing constant and watchful about me, the ceiling rippling and alive with motion above, it was as though he was once more beside me, his limbs wrapped snug about me, heavy with sleep. So that when it was time, I felt that in fact it was not me who was dressing in the laid-out clothes, nor me going quiet and calm down the narrow stairwell into the darkness beneath, but that it was in fact him, with me merely listening out for him, and watching him go.

It was the sight of his boots in the hallway beside mine that made me pause, though not through indecision. A sweetness stopped me there as I measured the large size of his feet against my own, turning from that sight at the thought of spiders now the sole inhabitants of those boots' toe-tips.

So I stood there dead still for a second while I breathed in deep the seashell scent of his coat, musted with its year of hanging there, unworn. I took care not to meet the sight of myself in the hallway mirror, listening rather to the sound of his woolly struggles as he found his hat, pulled it down just as I did around my ears, liking the roughness of new itches across my forehead. The turned-back cuffs of his shirt were buttoned about my wrists. His trousers, rolled up, were the ones belted about my waist. Upstairs there was nothing now but silence. The house was almost empty. I was nowhere: I had already left, with him now following after.

For sure, it was his hand that rested on the door handle, hesitant, though only momentarily, feeling the cool metal worn smooth with his cracked palm's familiar use, clasping and releasing it. His eyes were the ones that glanced back into the shadowed kitchen, left precisely as though he'd return to it at the long day's end. And the footfalls, too, quieter perhaps than his might've been, but still, I can see how it was his deliberate pace that troubled a lone gull, worried off its perch of sleep beneath an eave. The cough wasn't quite his. The tone was higher and thin with reluctance. His throat would've offered a sound almost joyous in the morning, a gulp of purest pleasure as he thought of the day now waiting.

I passed no one. Thinking of this, I imagine that most days he would've maybe met another in the street, headed likewise for the sea. And in fact, one day, I know for sure he did meet someone. Yes, now there's no pretending I didn't have a hand in things, my mind is ticking a restless tap against itself, remembering, not letting me forget. You know for sure he did meet someone, you know it, don't you, and what business have you pretending you've forgotten such a thing, when now there's not a soul on earth to see your shame?

Yes, it is such a simple thing – he has forgotten his

lunch. It falls from his bag as he leaves the house. I even hear it fall, a sullen thump onto stone that sends me rushing down to remind him. He's already gone, and I get dressed and tear out after him, careless of superstition that day because it started out so fine and lovely, with no threat of any kind to torment me in my curtain vigil, guessing at storms or dangerous seas. So yes, I am careless of the superstition there's been here for no one even knows how long, that says it's bad luck for a man to greet a woman in the street before he goes to sea. Men have stayed at home for less, refusing fate's temptation. But not him. I don't care for old wives' tales, that's what he says, laughing as he goes – though I can see the doubt faint-shadowing his eyes.

So we are over-bold and careless. And with his disbelief tied tight about my happiness, it is as though we think we hold some kind of talisman against all danger – that's how it feels. I remember this with the menace of a future wound. The thought's still granite-sharp within me.

I am out of breath by the time I reach him, and he is glad to set eyes on me again, grateful for my memory of his lunch. So he holds me, drops his bag and holds me in his rib-tight way till I am breathless and chock with longing for his return. And then I watch him go, his boots upon cobble much like mine as I tread the exact same path this morning, only more real somehow, as though resonant with the steps of years of similar footfalls, all harmonious and beckoning to be followed, so that in fact he isn't striding out to sea alone that day, but borne there by an orchestra of ancient sound, which lures him, seduces him, invincible siren-pull towards the ocean.

5

The sun has passed beyond dawn's scrim of sea mist now, lifting itself skywards and making gold of all the water. But still it offers no heat, only the lees of summer's sunlight, a cool dazzle that makes the land appear faint and pale as smoke, the entire length of coastline liable to an act of vanishing. And it's not that I'm finding it hard to see how I ever lived on such an insubstantial shade of air-like stuff, but that it's almost impossible to see how anyone at all might live in such a state – I'll not call it a place, because how can it be real, how can it count for everything when all you have to do is spy on it from a different angle to see how airy and how nothing it in fact is?

And is this the look I've seen in their eyes when

they've come back from the long trips? The look that is not distant so much as exclusive of all others, as though those nights spent out at sea have been passed in fact with their one true love and returning was done with guilt and keen reluctance? Because certainly there is something sorrowful-remote about their faces then, as though they'd been locked in an embrace with life itself, and yet been told to leave it – for what? For the dream of land?

Because looking back at it now, it seems composed of nothing more than that – just dreams and shade, some medallion weight of wonder they'd have to bear about with them, feeling its heaviness with dumbstruck disbelief and anguish, knowing in their hearts that all that was most real was in the ocean, a petulant flux that enthralled them, sorcerered them to its depths. For how can those on land insist to a man who has felt his life in motion that he stay rooted to the earth that way?

I have my eyes angled landwards as I turn off the engine. The silence is no silence whatsoever, though it seems profoundly empty of noise when first I taste it. Soon enough I discover otherwise, noticing the gunwale lappings like tiny tongues, urging the boat to a tide unfelt on the surface but boiling and writhing away far below no doubt, twitching upwards by unseen stealth. I can hear the sea-drops on the transom, pattering round the ungunned engine and gulping about the propeller shaft, slick with oil. There's a thin wind, too, audible only by its nudge against canvas, and by its whistling lisp past the taut-strung stays that keep the canvas tented. Overhead there are gulls, elegant on tricky thermals.

So I watch the vanishing land and wonder what it is to me now that I have unhooked myself from it. Is it even so much as memory? Because it's as though by leaving I'm unravelling the slender thread of my life behind me, casting it adrift on the water and watching it become broken up and frail, a thing it'd be impossible to haul myself back to shore with. All I can do is watch the snake-like sloughing off of all I've done and felt, everything that's been most near and close, now observed from this delicate remove of buoyancy, suspended as I am above unchallenged miles of motion uncontrollable.

And was it like this for him every time he set out to sea? Was I his landbound anchor? So maybe then he also guessed at the massive removal of faith that's imminent and dreadful on the abandoned tide, each time he watched the coast dissolve, hidden behind the more real mountains of the sea.

6

I can see him now as on the first day. I am nineteen and the year is at the high point of summer, the season not quite turned, and overblown with months of heat and the swollen scent of unshucked wheatfields, the meadow grass scorched across the clifftops, the roads transformed to bridal tunnels by swaying clouds of cow parsley, starred with nettle flowers that appear sparky amongst the ragged blue blooms of borage, sinking airless into brown.

He comes into the cool church smiling, wearing a suit too short and small to fit his length and breadth of limbs, and his face is faintly damp with sweating up the hill. His boots upon the stone are cumbersome though he is wanting them to be quiet – I can tell this by the way he seems to prance about to find his pew, as though fearful of the noise and not knowing it as his own. His hair is sunlit, the blondeness of it made ruby by the blood-stained light that angles through the glass. Shafts of uncut hair fall across his eyes until he wipes them clear of it, and the fine template of bones beneath the flesh of his face makes him seem like a child in a man's body, his nostrils widened with his uphill effort to get here just on time, his lips as rosy as two smooth mounds of Turkish delight, unbitten. He has perfect teeth. I catch a flash of them when he smiles at me as he sits down, and did he read each one of my thoughts about him then? My God, but I can think of nothing else but him throughout the service, travelling across his face in my mind's eye with a starvation panic of feasting.

Everything about him makes me smile and tremble with a sensation so mixed up and vast that I cannot haul one single word towards it to come close to saying what it is. I sit there turned away from him but I can see him after that one glance as perfectly as though I'd looked on him for years, his face statued, almost, from an elegance of marble that is given shape and form only by his emergence from it. It's as though until that moment I'd been holding my breath and only now am I able to follow up that gulped-in attempt at living with the steadiness of exhalation. My life has not been right until he entered it, I'm thinking to myself, relief honeying its way through my veins, a narcotic pleasure of rightness that I can barely believe is real. I must've been wrongly wired up before, I am grinning to myself.

But all my smiles are fleet-chased by a massive anger, feeling breathless, almost winded suddenly, as though he's thieved my life from under me before birth and now I'll have to fight him till he'll give me back that measure of myself. It's an outrage for him to be roaming about the place without me, is the way the sensation strikes me, making my skin feel hot and vulnerable, as though he'd drawn away mid-kiss to leap half round the world and make me miss him further by the quickness of his absence. It's all wrong for him to be so distant from me, I think to myself, there must be some kind of error that has kept this wrong so long unfixed.

I am facing the cross and the wedding couple's bent-necked promises but can see these things only as though they were the remotest facts, described to me in absolute darkness, with him the only thing lit up, the only thing of worth anywhere at all across the night-day twist of fast-spun earth, and thank God, I'm praying for sheer happiness, thank God, for this is more than luck for me to have found my love at last. And I sit still throughout that service only by an effort of politeness that later on I laugh at, as though all manners, every word of how we're told we should behave, sits sullen now and obsolete beside that craven necessity of being fast and soon beside him.

After the service I discover who he is: a cousin of some other cousin many times removed, who has been aiming here for years, or so I'm told, circumnavigating the globe on merchant navy ships, a satellite finding earth post-orbit. We are introduced by someone who smiles as they do it, looking from me to him and standing back slightly as though to set our match within the amber gleam of sight.

I have my eyes on his feet so that he cannot see my skin's warm flush, loving his feet and itching to put my own up on them to see how well they'll fit there, not daring yet to lift my eyes up to his face which is so beautiful I can feel it shining Phoebus-bright above me, certain to dazzle or be Medusa-ish, perhaps, and set my heart in stone forever after looking there.

He is repeating my name, slippering it so quietly, almost whispering it across his tongue as though he were kissing every syllable as he first pronounces it, sealing it that way with the rosy pressure of his lips. I feel snake-charmed by the sound of his voice, as though it were an opiate music I could forever stay succumbed to. And with my eyes lingering there on his lovely feet, and my name lassoed by him, inquisitive on his lips – no longer my name but a question: am I who he thinks I am? – I have the fact of *yes* re-flowing all the blood that's in me. When at last I risk a peek up at his eyes, they're widened with the curiosity of shock to meet my own, and can it be true that he has in his thoughts one small part of what I'm thinking? He blushes as he takes my hand in greeting, holding it there without release, his fingers slipping each one inside mine to nestle close against their secret roots and twine untamed about my wrists, sweet binding up of me to him.

I can feel the heat of his hip bones as they graze against my own and I spy on him from the corner of my eye, allowing myself tiny slices of him a little bit at a time because the sight of him is sharply precious as an antique blade of gold and I am sure of being cut just by the look of him, because what if the next time I peek he's become different? But I know that he will not have changed, that however many years of gazing on him, this moment of first seeing him will be set inside my heart, unshiftable. No, he will not change, and nor can I, as though our meeting is a kind of perfect locking tight of two imperfect parts. And it's then that I realise with absolute certainty that he is me and has already handed over everything of himself that I could ever crave, and that well before my ever setting eyes on him I had the empty space there waiting far within me, ready for him to enter there.

His shoulder is inches above my own, and as the sun falls beneath the rim of land behind the village, blackening the pine forests to a pitchy line of dark, it seems entirely natural for me to rest my head there. That's right, he whispers, and I can feel him smiling at me as he says this, comforted that he can offer comfort. His hand slides about my waist and the pressure of it confounds me: nothing in my life has ever felt so sure, so tender, nor so brightly electric as his presence alongside me, and I am certain I must be lit with shocks that anyone might see. But it is our secret: he looks, unflinching, at me, his eyes saying, Yes, I know, don't worry I can see you, and I feel the magnetic fizz of life inside his flesh-pressed fingertips that find their earth against my skin.

There is dancing on the beach until the stars tattoo the night, and a falcate moon casts silver on the sea. The air remembers sunshine from the August day, still rich and resonant in the heated earth, and the candlelight is alive with an uncertain sparkle of midges and gnats, catching the brightness of it like fireflies. We go knee deep in sea to dance, and kiss hours later in the shadow of the harbour wall. And though I can scarce believe it, thinking of it now, that night we see a shooting star. Both of us look up at the precise same second to see that dazzling, heaven-ish death. We tell no one. No one else notices. It is our sign, our promise, a stellar bolt of secrecy to bind us ever after.

7

The mist is lifting off the sea, leaving the surface of it glassy clean, as though the water has just licked it so. The colour of it is inky blue, a dense completeness of pigment that looks as though it might swallow what part of yourself you're fool enough to dip there. I can see myself reflected in it when I lean over the side – at least, there's some lone stump of darkness there, jumping to the beat of a shore-drawn tide. And isn't that how it was for us? Trust me, he'd say, cajoling with his welkin eyes, leap right in and I'll not harm you, I'll keep you tight and warm beside me, never be leaving you. Leaving one another is not for us now, is it? And what do you make of me that I'd ever think to do such a thing as that?

He washes himself across me as he speaks, and I am tenderised with strokes and kisses, glances that charm me into trust, words like ointment on my fear. So I jump in and give him all, peel myself ripely like an autumn-heavy fruit, dropping for sheer pleasure to his palm. I open every box of panic I possess and hand him the key, entirely glad to do it – unable to do otherwise. His eyes have scraps of sky within them, bright luminosity of blue, and I am airborne there, seeing the freedom that might come of such unmasking of myself. And then he holds me closer than before, until faith, like the miraculous generation of a diamond, grows ever more between us till we are tight with love, unshatterable.

We are on a clifftop – I remember this with perfect clarity, so sharp it makes me wince now to remember it, like my heart is being pinched by impish nails intent on hurt – when we first talk about the years ahead. He'll be giving up the sea, he tells me. Meeting me has done it for him and he's happy that way, liking, almost, that silly vision of his younger self awash and roguish with nautical indiscretion, now reneged upon. That life's all done with, is how he puts it; how do you suppose it'd be even possible to be away from you, now that I've found you? To prove this logic, he moves still closer, our skin matching in the clifftop air, busy with gulls and the boom of cavernous seas beneath the scrag miles distant – or so it seems when we press our bellies to the turf and peek there, terrified at the height of ourselves.

There's an uncle with a farm nearby. He'll be sure to need an extra hand, so what'll be better than that? He jokes about turning tiller skill to tilling skill, the furrows to be his ocean – and I'm laughing alongside him, holding to his lips ripe pippins scrumped and lovely.

From here the village is visible only as an ascending plume of smoke, and the sky is as huge as though we were in flight. The fossil-packed cliffs below us seem unimportant, weighted with no history we'll ever be called upon to measure our small lengths against. Right through my lungs I can smell the peaty worm-turned soil and the tang of tall grass, and it is impossible to conceive the depth of effort rolling on beneath, as though we're borne along by our own will entirely, and by no other's. Waiting, that day, is happiness, because it is all expectation and clear-sightedness.

The sun is in our eyes and so we often shut them, talking as though we walk in sleep, all meaning wrapped within the faith of dreams. It is late in the year and that sunshine is a gift. The grass itches my exposed back and he tickles it with a speckled cormorant feather, dropped from the wing. We see no one else for hours. A cyclist passes and a woman with an unleashed dog calls the beast away when she spies us twined together like fighting cats in the uncut meadow grass, thick with full-blown thistles and buttercups long since crisped with heat.

When we leave, there is an imprint there, the grass flattened, the flowers smashed. Our cheeks are pink after kissing, and the air is growing cooler with the sinking sun. I'm gathering up our things, rolling a rug, tipping away cold tea, when I catch him staring. He is standing on the edge of the cliff, his toes seeming almost to curl over the edge like a high-wire act of horrible skill. I watch him. I do not dare to shout or speak a word, afraid that with one syllable I might send him rockwards, see him scraping the air with savage hands. His eyes are lit and wonderful. His brow is calm, with a kind of devastating loveliness upon it, the skin all soft, unrucked with trouble. His left hand is raised and wrapped about his waist, clutching at his guts as though his soul is burning, restlessly aflame with pleasure. There is a sudden rightness in his posture that I've never seen before. There he is, I think – that's him right now, not the one I've seen before but this person now, exactly as he appears to me this moment and no other.

He is looking at the sea. His eyes are on the horizon. I follow his gaze to see whatever on earth he can be looking at. What is it that is holding him so transfixed and desolate? I can see nothing. There is nothing there that I can see. There is only the ocean, falling into shadow at the close of day. When he turns back to me I can see he has been grieving. His eyes implore me, begging me to let him be the man he is.

8

The land is nothing but a slim line of distant silver now that the little boat has inched towards the horizon, powered by no engine save the sea's mysterious cauldron of tides, witching me away from shore as though I were in thrall to a spell unspoken. The dazzle from the sun has glazed the sea to a cracked pool of ever breaking ice, reflecting fire at a low angle that pierces my eyes and makes me squint against its brightness. No, I cannot believe in land any more – I'm smiling as I think this, remembering that look of his that told me how he'd never belong there, stuck among soil on the clifftop farm, but that he'd be pulled like flotsam on each descending tide, down into the unfathomable deep well of the sea, ever lowering, forever drawing him closer to itself.

He wasn't a man to lie, though for my sake he tried to do it: he worked at that uncle's farm for an entire year. I watched his face grow swarthy with a glum stupidity of mud that did not suit him. He'd return home low-shouldered with defeat, and often I'd see him become restless, fingers drummed in envy at a friend's description of their trip to sea. I'd watch the way he'd clutch his pint in anguish, hating them, wanting to be out there too, rocked into himself by the sea's incredible motion, the agile trick that'd soothe him back into the skin of himself like nothing else. He'd even grow mournful at the sight of fish at Friday dinnertime, asking how I'd come by it, and chewing it with sombre, desirous grinds of his strong, white teeth, his eyes flickering across the closed curtains of the window as though distracted by the hidden noise of ocean, ponderous and insistent beyond the refusing hang of chintz.

There is talk of it before I know for sure, and then one day he comes back with a tidy, tiny heap of notes and tells me: the farm has laid him off. There is hardship there, and no work to be had. He tries to look apologetic as he tells me, but his eyes are an invocation as he talks of men he knows right along the coast who cannot beg for work since there is not one job to spare for those untrained for it, nor any for those who have the skills that are sought after. I'm only fit for one thing, he states, and casts his eyes floorwards as he leaves the room.

I stay below, wringing my hands, looking down at them with a kind of wonder, realising it is a thing I've never even seen before, barely thinking that hands can in fact perform that abject gesture – yet it's true, and I watch my own hands writhe and twist in amazement, dread, until I hear him sink against the springs of the bed which stands beneath the window. And by that sound I know that for near on an hour he's been standing there, doing nothing except gaze out at the sea. He does not cry but tears are there in the way he sinks, humiliated, to the bed, and when I go up after him he turns the moment he hears me, holding out his hand.

You don't need to ask me, I tell him, feeling the seasick grip of anguish swollen up inside me, seeming to pierce right through my heart and flood my veins with pity, as though my blood divines right then what harm will come to him. I watch him hunched there, gilded in the afternoon's last light, and I miss him with such pain it is not bearable, as though in fact he's not sitting warm and safe before me but is already miles beneath the damaging waves, tumbled within the vast oppression of the sea which will rob him of all breath, and bloat his skin, his guts and heart, so that he cannot catch hold of life but only have it snatched fast and ever faster from him.

I am hate-filled at this moment, as never before or since. Had I been godlike I would've dreamed up curses unimaginable, draining the sea of all its drops until it was dried up, arid and repulsive, with not a speck of life left to it. I'd have made it impossible, a thing no more than fantastical, that he should ever go to sea except in dreams that would mean nothing more than wonder when he awoke, marvelling at them with laughs, his eyes rolled and barely curious as he turns again to me and, landlooked, we embrace in safety.

No, love, you don't need to ask me, I tell him, watching him trying not to cry for sheer relief – it is not happiness, but something more like a profound content, or maybe dignity, as though the sea is a debt he owes his soul, and so he wouldn't have felt honourable had he gone on a single other second of neglecting it. He holds me tight then, with my face safe-buried in his neck, because he knows it won't be fair to let me see his eyes' flickering gleam of absolute want, trammelled seawards like a twine of copper wire, keeping him electric-set and vital. No, it wouldn't have been fair to let me set my eyes on that. And from that day on, there is a slender thread between us, broken.

Remember the shooting star? he asks, still clutching me blind against him. It is our invocation, the thing we say to haul the other to us. But now those words are like a knife well-aimed to wound: I remember exactly that shooting star. It was a kind of promise – no, there is no word to fit this – it was a sort of declaration that we were bound by chance, by whatever it is that triumphs, redemptive, in the face of all the thousand years that say it can't be so. Because we have had great nets of despair to rip through – he knows as well as I. It has always been the way, throughout my family. When the men go out to sea they die. And who are we to pit ourselves against that fate?

So the only remedy is to avoid – I know this is the only chance we have – to stay here landbound, our backs to the ocean, defying its keen thievery of time.

Because every woman along my family's tree of history has suffered by the sea. And why will he and I be any different? I want to bawl this in the foxglove softness of his ear to remind him of the thing I thought he understood. He knows the facts of how I am, the dangers near-encroaching on my mind, so how can he now neglect to care for what they mean? Because however many skins of centuries are torn through, excavating time and trouble like a maniac intent on proof, still, the same terrible treasure will be unearthed.

And yet there's more to it than this, since in the back room of my heart a kind of pride is spiked there now, indignant. Because I had almost thought that by our love we'd slipped right off that fatal wheel, our lives re-scored to a different music – an entirely private, precious thing, far distant from the drumbeat thunder that runs like bloodshed down the eastern coast. I know the sound, the hateful pound of fear unquenchable in my family's blood. I can see the hordes of women on the shore, staring at the blankness of a sea that'll spit out nothing for them but broken wood, oftentimes bearing their husband's legend in fabulous paintwork – the faint monikers like bad talismans that do not work against disaster. *Faithful, Lady, Darling, Beloved*, and all the names of wives, too, as though to taunt them on their return, bearing no man home.

Yet I had started to think maybe we were different, though now I see the life that lies in store. My mother, her mother, countless daughters and sisters throughout my family have all suffered this inevitability. The sea has opened wide its mouth and their men have fallen in without a sound.

And do you not remember that it's a tradition hereabouts, I want to whisper at him as reminder of the price, for men to carry beach stones in their oilskin pockets? Do you not know of this? It makes them more efficient drowners. They suffocate then in moments, not enduring the vile attenuation of existence that comes of North Sea hypothermia. No, that'd be rash, pretending there is hope when they know that there is none. So they wear stones in their pockets, for the love of God, and is that the way I'm going to let you go each morning, with an offering of stones and what great faith that you should ever come back alive?

But I say nothing to him then, nor ever once resist his choice. For who am I to fight against this weight of time? His own family have all lived long and ancient. It is my family that bears the curse, and he'll remain exempt from it, for sure he will. But I don't try overhard to balance upon this lie, either to myself or him. I cannot make myself believe it. I can hear the truth of what will happen in my veins, it pulses so strong, as though the blood is roaring with a deep and winter tide I'll not contain with wishing it were otherwise.

Thank you, he is murmuring with his lips still warm against my throat, tripping along the thin skin of my jugular with a carelessness that makes my heart go numb, thumped to a guttered stop inside my chest. Thank you with all my heart, he says. And you'll forgive me?

My kiss is his absolution but I cannot offer the blessing that he is eager for. It isn't there to give him. I am too afraid. Even more afraid, nudging at a kind of desolation, to hear him offering something I'll never find the blindness to have faith in now, as he whispers against my ear, his words seeming already to mingle with the worn-out waves upon the shore, only yards, so close, from our bedroom window, open to allow the salt-sharp breeze to enter with a stealth I want to rail against, knowing its intrusion is final – because his words are my future, a drowned impossibility that I listen to as from a distance too remote for sound, only the echo of an unfelt intent, as he tells me things I no longer dare believe. How can I? The fear is blotting out the light of all my night-safe dreams of happiness.

And he knows this. In his guts he knows the worry lurks there for us both. That it will take an effort of will it is impossible to conceive if we are ever to have a chance of half the life we've both been hankering after, since now he's set a part of himself aside from me, and asked me still to live as carefree-sure as ever in the citadel we have conjured up, fantastical pearly-gated playground for our hearts to be forever childed in. Because it's just not possible, he's telling me now by this decision, for us to make-believe we're any different from the rest of the world. Our love is the illusion, the thing that happens out of time. And now we must obey the hooked-up tidal logic of the sea.

He is still lip-pressed against me as he slips me fishlike from my dress, and holds me naked and beneath him, watching me as though expecting something secretively changed. I cannot bring my eyes to meet his, as though to use up even one superfluous moment of gazing on him will be to hurry ever closer that now soon and frozen moment when he'll be unreachable and miles gone from me on the ocean, far distant by no other wish than his.

The dusk has crept like smoke beneath the curtain, filling the room. He seems unfamiliar, and uneasy with my sadness. And for the first time I resent the fact that I am naked here beneath his fallen gaze, wishing he could not see me thus cast out and needful of the Edened place we were before.

He holds me tight and tender, and my sorrow is shot through with guilt, despising itself, longing not to feel so wrought with anguish at this simplest of decisions he has made. He's only going out to sea as thousands of others have done before him. So why am I being so foolish, believing always the worst, as though my fear were prophecy, not just the fear itself, and negligible, surely, if ignored?

And it is no use chastising myself with secret

threats, I tell myself, because already I can smell the seabed wreckage on his breath, as though my kisses were the unreturnable kisses into a life already drawn out from his body, his limbs limp and grey upon the shingled beach, with me bent over him and blowing in his lungs to bring him back to life in vain. I know this is how it will be as surely as though it happened many broken years ago, had long since turned to chip-shop newspaper, remarked on by a friend: I'm so sorry, love, it must've been heartbreaking, how did you manage?

But pressing close and warm around me, he is covering me in a sincerity of love I cannot shrink from. He has words to jewel me in temporary hopefulness, telling me, There's no need for fear. You're mine and I'm entirely yours, so there's no room between for trouble, or fear. Do you see how this is true? And with him so precious near me, it seems undeniable that this is so. Though could I pay for proof of this one fact I'd sell my soul to do it, since I'm wishing like a fool that every word he utters was a rope so I could bind him safely close against me, and that way let him stray no further from me than he is right now.

So then when we're old together, he's whispering against my skin, his lips brimmed over with invitations hotly offered for me to fall inside his faith, We'll sit together on the clifftops if we can still make it there on creaky legs, and we'll think on this time and smile like seadogs both, remembering how it was hard but that we endured it, and came through great years of me at sea, and look at us now, two old ones still so happy because still so true. And no harm can come to me because of our star, remember? So there'll be no harm. No harm, do you see?

But the dusk has snaked through all the small room's light until it is evening absolutely now, and soon enough the night, where I can see nothing much beyond the faint pale tussle of our limbs, pungent with new sweat like just-cracked clamshells, divulged from under massive weights of sea.

9

The sky is pitted white against the massed black waves, with the sun barely visible behind a heavy pall of cloud. I can feel the surreptitious turbine curl of tides beneath the skin of the water, sending vibrations profound and inquisitive up through the thin wooden boards of the little boat's hull. It's warmish within the air now that the coastal mist has lifted skywards, vanishing into the denser plains of white, so that my face feels pleasant, calm against the tickling breeze that's uncertain-seeming about which way to turn.

I take my boots off and put my thick-socked feet out flat on the bilge boards, liking the nervous thrum of water licking along the wood below. I can sense the life of the boat that way, or so it seems, as though the blood is running easy and harmonious through the bentwood planks it's fashioned from. It's a craft that feels pliable, agile, as though it can be pressed and curved around a thousand fisted hands of angry seas and yet survive it still, for being elusive, changing its shape to fit the greater will, without resistance.

She's an old boat, bought off a fisherman without any sons. The omen, we decided, was a good one – it would carry whoever sailed in it to safety throughout whatever length of years. I do not think on this for long. I admire instead her clinker-built flanks, the tight-knit ribs of wood that make her fierce and true against all leakage. She's painted white, with a sky-blue trim. The job is fresh done. Only last week I sweated on it in the harbour, spawning questions, answered with a lie: I'm thinking of selling her, I told all askers, who seemed to understand. Why indeed, they agreed, would his wife ever wish to keep that fatal boat?

I turn aside from this thought as from a hurt, inflicted without sense or purpose. How would they be expected to know what drives me now? No, they've not a clue. And there's comfort there, a richness of comfort, I tell myself, setting my shoulders against the rising wind that's still warm but strengthening. The surface of the sea is blemished with squalls that gust and disappear in moments. They raise no spume, merely darkening the water like footsteps in wet sand, dissolving. But I can feel the shape of the swell along my backbone. Between the vertebrae, there's an irregular shuddering, hitching motion as though each bone is being cajoled to suppleness.

Time now is measured in degrees of difference, and every hour the day grows less familiar. The air smells as though it has been washed clean by risen spray, so fine I can see only the sheen of it refracting light. Some way distant, the sea's shaded monochrome is brushed with tiny white-capped waves. But it's impossible even to guess at distance, and those waves could be the gossamer descent of gulls.

Now there are no more reminders of the land to lag about on thermals, terrorising me with yearning for a thing that can't be had. The sea is all there is and I breathe it in, a deep breath bearing with it sinuous slips of oil and diesel, damp wood and sunbleached canvas, the faintest scent of last night's rain upon the paintwork, and beneath, above, wrapped right around the whole of it, the perpetual lushness of airborne salt that seems as natural now as air itself.

Yet still there's the unblinking separation of the sea and sky, sliced in two by a horizon visible only as the line of nothing that divides them. And it is just this way when he leaves the first time. I have the memory of that day silted up inside my mind, precisely as it settled there.

There is a raw spring tide that carries him and twelve others out the harbour mouth, their frail oak masts set like crosses dark and hopeless against a sky that contains no colour whatsoever. I can still see how those black wands seem to scratch out hieroglyphs against white canvas, transcribing the same weird script of faith in the face of all blankness and all negation. The women, and me among them, stand busy and low-voiced upon the seafront, though I am sure I'll not be able to bear it for a second beyond this moment, seeing in their soft acceptance a flatness of unchange and separation that I will not put my name to.

I remember how I stand for a time when they're all gone, alone, watching the boats drawn like magnets far out to the deep water, smoke-grey blots that seem to hover and speculate like doves against the black, pausing against it as they set their nets, floating them far down beneath the surface of the water to lurk there almost as icebergs might, though visible by the warning bobs of a hundred tiny floats, dancing amongst the wrinkling ruck of waves – in and out of view like clues to danger. And above, the sky stays white, unanswering.

I stand there, restless with rage and silence, forced into a position I cannot accept: it goes against every drop of blood within me, as though somehow in the sneak of night he'd made me sign a pact that by day he knew I'd not agree to, saying, From this moment on, you'll no longer be my one love, but must share me with a sea that's rife with mystery, a thousand tales you'll never hear of – though maybe I'll let you know some of them one day, second-hand. I feel as though he's declared me different and apart from him in a way I know we aren't, that in fact we are not pitted like opposing forces, one hard against the other, but that we are merged, re-emergent, indivisible. And who is he to try to say it's otherwise?

Seeing him slice out across the sea is like listening to him shout denial in my face, telling me that he does not know me, that I belong away from him, on land. So I watch the sea and wait, hating that fact of waiting, looking up at the thunderous crumble of cliffs which stand against the sea like a patience that I'm unable to feel. I want to be snake-like, cunning and quick to follow him, slip out along the water to surprise him with a mermaid kiss that will prove everything: You don't belong so far away now, do you? You should be near, and in my arms, right out of danger and distant from the curse that'll claim you. But he does not hear me. He is deaf to my calling him, although all that day I cry and crave him.

Yet I had wanted us to meet in somewhere secret, between ourselves, a place where we could stay like children without words, with virgin hearts so close we'd never grow to be two polar points of difference, leather-skinned and ancient with long habits of denial, admiring one another across a depthless stretch of ocean. I want to be out there in that boat with him, not stuck passive on the shore of life, a spectator of our separation.

Now the whiteness of the sky has made hot milk of all the sea, the infinite series of waves ending nowhere. Even the boat itself is bathed in the blankness of vapours, and the thought of dropping anchor is absurd: the iron hook would catch on nothing. There would be no soundings, no muffled thump of certainty, no echo of anything but itself.

So what does it matter which direction I take? Each way is equal, and similarly devoid of sense. I have made him my life, and this is the price: to have lost my bearings with his absence. Now, all I have left is my own diminishing will to remember, a solitary voice trying to listen to itself for no other purpose than to recover what love was once contained there, hidden within the now-dead decibels of language.

It is no good to me to think that parallel lines meet at some point, somewhere, in infinity. That will not do. How could it, when I have him still so present and within me? As though his blood still pounds inside me to my heart's own beat, tapping against the paradise place that we once knew the way that thieves know luxury – handling it like jewels in the dark, telling it by touch and faith, and sharing eyes to understand our luck.

Because later, when he returns, and I have him close and skin-bared beside me, it seems a fact impossible to dispute – that we are somehow one, two parts of the same new bud of flesh and need, now opening like a kind of summertime thing, all ripe and wanting union, gloating after the honey-bee's dart and slippery drip of pollination. He wrestles me against him as we stagger upstairs, drunk with an urgency of sea-fever eagerness that bucks and tips our legs till we can no longer stand but fall, happy drowners, to the bed.

No, it was not true that we were separate. We did not love in opposition but with some strain of harmony gouged from miles of shifting water to pour upon us, cool with blessing. I feel the nervous hum of the miles-deep sea beneath, transmitted like secret signals through the ancient wood. And could it be that he is out here? I shut my eyes, feeling him beneath me now, a fine vibration of remembrance that seems so near it could be future, almost, not yet past, as though if I can keep myself held like this, above and on it – neither past nor future, so much as both at once – then I'll be fixed to find him here, plumb the deep to steal him from the past's dark grave of memory.

Why can I not do that? I ask myself, feeling the sun already start to fall slow from the low point of the sky where, almost autumn-caught, it has been resting. Why can I not turn archaeologist in time and dig him up from what far place he's hidden? For he's all my past, my now, and future, too, because where else can he be but in my heart, remembering? So then he's here, incarnate, and that way I will find him, exhume him from myself, divide him flesh from soul and hold him here till my death quenches memory and then there will be nothing – but that's not yet.

I open my eyes to see that the sea is thick with darkness more than ever now, and the sky is grown somewhere beyond the paleness of its muted blue, stretching to be like the nothingness that must've been before all opposition first began – before there was either a past or future to consume us in either memory or anticipation, when we could have lived in some loved suspension of the swollen moment, a thing more than enough, without the need for either a falling back, or a reaching forwards, just a steadiness there forever. So that on this fragile boat, shining silverish as a wily fish flashing by the fading day, it's as though I'm nothing more than a scrap of spirit, or perhaps imagination nakedly itself, slipping through the needle-eye place that's in between, with the two weights hanging sonorous and sure against each other, above, below, and just letting me through so delicate and easy, as though I were a thing fantastical, a granted wish.

For sure, he's not gone, not even nearly, I am smiling, my skin soft and taut as though he held it, caressingly, against his own. Because we were never either black or white, nor sea and sky, nor even man and woman. We were the place between.

10

It's only when I angle full round to face where I guess the land used to be that I understand just what the day is doing. The empty white is now gleamingly so, an unflat arch of paleness like a mirror's reflection of a vast and boatless lake of silver, shivery with a timbre of motion almost musical so that I half expect to catch hold of the sound of its secret harmony. The air seems hurried, as though speeded through teeth. It appears to grow cooler with every forward motion and I imagine icebergs lurking just out of sight beyond the horizon, an inky freeze that flowers the dark like blotting paper. I pull my hat further down towards my eyes and flex my mittened fingertips, feeling the frailty of the bone, the skin stretched sore with the start of chilblains around my knuckles.

The waves are not high but they are hard, slapping against the prow as though to turn the boat about and send it back to land, towards the place where there's still some remnant of the day. I can feel the resistance in the muscles of my shoulders as I hunker down deeper inside my coat, wriggling my toes for heat. The sea is twitching now with uncertain bolts of brightness, restless with opalescent shades of violet and gold, and turning back towards the west I see the reason why: a massive yellow sun has slipped from its concealment of clouds, and is falling even now behind the just-seen silhouette of remaining land, blackening it to a filigree of unpolished jet, sucking all the life out from the light.

I have the engine gunned, and I'm glad of its banal and pointless chug, almost wishing I could drown the beauty of the setting sun, as though it were an orchestra that I might shout over. Because it is too opulent with itself, too full of riches that it seems senseless to leave unsung – the whole world casually gorgeous with the gift of itself, making it absurd that I should be looking at it alone, from this articulate viewpoint, and how can I deserve such luck as this? I feel almost humiliated by it, as though I have no part in it, as though I am a spy.

But still, I cannot keep my eyes off it, watching the sun dip to its death behind the land, slow and sure, with not a pause in its descent that'd give me some hope that there wasn't an order in things, some force, malign, that said life must be so, and so, and fixed in a pattern of logic that I can't abide, not any longer. Because it *is* malign, despite its beauty, I know this now for sure. How could it not be so, since I am so alone? And it would take a mammoth leap of faith to trip me off this track, the one I'm glued to since there is no other. At least, not one I can believe in any more, though for so long now, I swear, I've tried.

The water all about me is bleeding and tremulous, seeming suddenly fragile, and the land has become no more than a charred twig of charcoal, obscure relic beneath the massive weight of light. I think of the people there, falling horizontal as each night dictates, just keeling over to some blind order they'll not question. I can see them now, all those I've left behind, quiet and uninquiring beneath their roofs before sleep.

I see the disputes and the intimacies, the worn grooves of familiar content that let them slip through years of chattered acquiescence, until such day as the world reminds them, do not be so bold, and with a silent snap prematurely breaks off their thread of life, silencing them in sea.

This has been the way throughout my family – for my mother, her mother, sister, cousins. And along the echo-troubled street, how many other times have footsteps brought the news?

It is deep wintertime with my father. A heavy tide has carried ice from unseen floes that've sailed down here from Greenland – I remember this particularly: it is the first time I've ever heard of Greenland, perplexed at the mention of it. What would somewhere turfy be sending ice down here for? I imagine little impish devils up there, chipping ice blocks with malicious hammers just to harm my dad. We are wellingtoned and wrapped up tight against the dripping sky, blowing sleety gusts of purest flu to wriggle down our necks and make us squirm. There's been a freeze inland, and it has hardened up the beck where we are playing, hacking at the icy stuff with sticks about the stepping stones that cross from north to south of it. There is some kind of war being staged, and I am in the middle.

It is almost night. There is a sulphur sheen of lamplight on the glugging water, bright and clear, bearing no mud because of the frozen earth beneath, which sheds nothing and makes the liquid luminous and dazzling. We've paused in play to crack some ice and eat it, wanting lollipops – and it is then I see her.

She hardly ever leaves the house around this time. She's always inside beside the stove, a schoolbook in one hand, spoon in the other. Dinner takes as long to cook as English homework does for her to mark, and I'm convinced our eating runs in tandem with the standard of the work. Good grades receive a smile and scented flourish, with delicious food revealed like tricks from the blazing oven. My dad often boasts of it, slipping an arm about her and tweaking her somewhere us children cannot see, to make her screech. In the morning all the exercise books are fragrant, slightly steam-curled at the edges.

Now she is standing there on the thin bridge that runs across the beck. She does not call to me, nor wave. She is alone. I should have been back home perhaps an hour before, but she is not angry. She is not large that way, nor full of motion and bluster. She is very small, and still, and silent. I go to her. She pulls me close against her and she is steady as she embraces me like a soft wall I've just walked into which has enveloped me. She wraps her coat about me as she used to do when I was very little – I am seven when this happens – and she stands like that not saying anything, while beneath us in the beck, my friends still whoop and splash about. I know that what they are doing is wrong, an inappropriate thing entirely, but I cannot speak to make them stop, as though her wordlessness is catching.

As we stand there, a boat comes under the bridge from off the sea. The canvas on it is ripped and flying, and I imagine that a giant claw has reached inside to scratch its guts out. The lobster pots are smashed. There is a fender missing, and one of the men has a cut, bleeding, on his cheek. The crew looks up at us and says nothing. All three of them take off their hats and stare ahead. My friends fall silent. My mother and I go on up to the house.

There were seas like Durham Cathedral, she tells me so I'll understand, and what boat would stand a chance in storms like that? We are lucky – she lies, I can see the lie in every muscle on her face – that any of them have come back alive today. And that is how we'll have to think of it, she says, her nails digging into my palm so I nearly cry out with hurt. We'll have to think of it as God's own will, and of how much worse it might have been, and that we'll be selfish if we go mad with sorrowing over such a thing because it has happened so many times before and will do so again, and there is nothing to be done about it, so we have to use our heads, this is how she puts it, and not our hearts.

But she is a liar. She doesn't mean one word of what she says. And all that night, and then for every night of my remembered childhood, I hear her praying in a way that is strewn about with tears through every verse of every psalm she utters. She knows it is not God's will, just as I know it now. Because is it God's will that says I should be without a father, and her without a husband? For what good reason should it be so? I ask her this one Sunday, after church that I've been dragged to with muttered curses. And what kind of sap does she take me for, that I'll believe those lies still further?

It is the only time she raises her hand against me. A swift clip to the back of the head when I tell her I consider it bloody foul lies to say that we should endure this without complaint. What, as though we deserve it? So then your own mother deserved it too? And why are you not spare with grief at having lost both father and husband? What's wrong with you that you have stayed so neat in the face of this injustice? Have you no heart left, Mother, is that it? And what about the fucking cousins? This is when I get the slap. We do not speak of it further.

The sea is deeply rosy with a wine-ish hue that looks impossible, until you stare. Then sense seems to be defeated, because sure enough, it is entirely so, a richness of colour still being blood-let from the sunken sun, now down beneath the land, which itself is bent on vanishing so that I'm utterly alone here, just as I'd wanted, and just as I'd aimed to be.

But I cannot get it from my head: the vision is stuck here now, of my father's limbs and ribs being pulverised by cathedral stones, his skin grazed by jewelled crosses and hunks of sacred rock. It's how I dream of it for years. I'd see him snug beneath the curling quilt of waves, suffocating there amongst the weed and glass shards that gather, later, upon the beach. Carried there exactly how? I want to know. By the kicking arms and legs of the drowning fishermen, who dash them back against the shore in recompense for the landbound ignorance that's sent them out there to look for death? Yes, I'm sure that's how it happens and my heart is queasy just to think on this.

Amen? I will not have it. Who says it must be so? I damn the one that did and in the sneak of my childhood night I take a razor blade and ribbon all the innards of my Bible. It is my father's razor blade. I know how he'd have smiled to see me do it, knowing that I've understood and will not lie down like the others, tombed before their time, but that I'll fix myself against the sky and stay land-rooted, growing there, not hurl myself upon the mercy of the sea, which does not care – why should it? – but is in fact pure mercilessness, which means only one thing: there is no God, no goodness ever likely to prevail, and why on earth now should there be?

Because what am I? My hands are shaking, the sweat making them slip and stutter against the tiller, which is restless with the engine's effort against my palms. I am alone, on a small boat, sailing into nowhere. And if there were something, somewhere, that I could head to and that way find the sense to things, then I would find it, since my life depends on it. But there is nothing. Only this blood-let trouble of sea and sky, and me no more than a floating boat on the rounded surface of things. Because if there were some power, some kind of God, then why would he make fishermen, fathers, sons, *husbands* die, who've done no harm to speak of? So then there is no God, because he cannot want it to be ordered so. Or maybe it's that he has no power to make it otherwise – and what kind of a God is that? So then yes, this is what it comes to. Either he's an evil God, or a good God without the strength to do a thing but sit and look, as impotent as I am – so then no God at all. What other answer could there be? Where is the way between?

My eyes are burning now with the beauty of the sea, which does nothing but taunt me with its effortless charms. The sky is paling and shot with the day's last brightness, and the sea is still sanguine-lit so rich it seems like precious stones that I could walk on, if I chose. Yes, I tell myself, this is all the truth there is, just what I can see within the little circle of my own two eyes – there's nothing else. There's only the incessant division between sea and sky, torn to a fierce red gash by the circled sun. Look how it cuts its way through all equations that the earth might offer.

So there is no suffering that's not explicable thus – in this abject acceptance of absolute nothing, seeing only what is, not what was or will be, or even what might have been. Just this, right now, and why should there be anything other than what I am? I look about me, asking this, the wind now cooler against my face, though only by the merest key, and still the driven astonishment banked up about me like the world's first snow. But is this how we die? Drowning in a beauty such as this?

11

I have the dusk in my eyes, with what breeze there was now hushed to a fragile lisp of wind that could be no more than my motion through it. Sound seems evanescent, fizzing towards silence. Beneath the steel-capped keel there's the chuckle and rush of water, goaded out behind by the submerged motor which makes a noise for me to hang my bearings on – a monotonous rope of sound. There is nothing else. The sun is long since horizon-sunk, casting no light beyond the palest pearl of not-quite-darkness. It is a pale night now, rather than a dark day – the two things no longer intertwined but definitely separate: already there are stars, and a new moon that corrals brightness in one corner of the sky, towards the north.

A layer of wetness seems to have slunk up off the surface of the sea to dew me in a net of damp, so I slough on an oilskin and tighten my scarf against the cold, wondering about the approaching night. The starlight seems twitchy, almost reversible, as though at any moment the stars will in fact not brighten but be snuffed out by a sudden cut of wind. There is no sight of land, only sea, with no sign of any other boats upon it. And am I the only one?

Up front in the bows, I have two small drums of diesel, squatting there as ballast, snug beneath the canvas awning. See, I have a way out, I remind myself, imagining the red flare's suddenness to ash. But I know the tricks my mind was playing to make me bring them with me, and their look of safety spells only cowardice. What was it that I ever hoped for?

I can see nothing. Only dusk. And does that count? Does the absence of day count for anything graspable, or am I really here alone, and that an end to it? There must be boats out there somewhere, I figure, screwing up my eyes and rotating steadily round like a lighthouse. But there is nothing. No sign of any kind of life, not even the night-path of an aeroplane to offer distant evidence.

I turn the engine off and the space sucks shut around me, wrapping me up in sea and sky and night and nothing more than that. With no relic of an other life anywhere on the horizon or in the sky, without even sunlight as reminder of the land's location, I am reduced in an instant to nothing more than a solitary woman in a fragile boat, rocked towards night on a slippery heave of sea. I can turn about in a survey of all the space I'm offered and my eyes are filled with the exact same thing – a calm harmony of emptying shade, shot through with tiny shards of starlight.

Shouldn't this feel different to anything I've felt before? I ask myself, curious. I should feel some kind of extreme isolation, surely, or new shock of smallness, fear. But it is no different to the exact same flow of feeling I've had since the day he last went to sea: a loneliness so extreme I'm always in search of another word for it, one that might hook itself up to this sense of separation from everything that once offered me a route right into life, fixing me up to things in a way that now I can only wonder at. Because is that what love did – gave me my life? My eyes feel sore to phrase this thought, remembering exactly the silence after he left, the emphasis of death articulate as the worst kind of fear, my voice calling out in the darkness, unanswered: *Are you there?*

I try to say his name, and I cannot do it, cannot frame the fact of any word at all. See, language cannot even rub up close to this feeling. I imagine describing it better with a wield of sound or colour, something inhuman and without the pretence of literal accuracy, a tangible metaphor as mirror to my loneliness. But I cannot do it. Because in the beginning there were no words, and that mute state of understanding sits like light inside my heart, however much I've armoured it over with ever greater tricks of language, pretending I might shut its golden mouth up with a phrase of hurt. No. I've not been able even to come close to doing this. It is too dazzling. And here's the proof, everywhere all around me.

Because alongside love, I have the last year of his absence blazing always in me, a terminal commotion that I cannot hitch up to any kind of chariot of words and that way bear it off, watch it vanish skywards. Losing him was just like this – every jot of emptiness I can see right now, multiplied, made endless, the veil between *I* and all other things so effortlessly ripped apart. Often, I would wake alone at night and feel precisely as I feel right now: a soul-felt fear of the sea. And when morning came, I'd try to bandage up that silence with a busy net of words entirely futile when set for just one second against the thing that most I feared – *this*, the ungraspable, language-less stuff of life.

But it was in the evenings that the worst ghosts came. I'd hear the sound of voices in the street outside, the ripples of emotion like fragments of a story that I should have known but could not bring myself to name: other people's happiness was remote, extraordinary, but still close enough a reminder of everything I'd lost that to forget meant only banishment. So for hours I would sit there beside the window, watching the figures passing by beneath the yellow glaze of streetlight and I'd conjure him, wondering at the cadences of subtle fights and laughter in the dark. Is that how we used to sound? And were there other listeners even then, similarly curious at their removal from life, hearing it humming by without them – and do they bear our imprint still upon them?

Sometimes, I would leave the front door unlocked throughout the night and make my sleep an act of waiting. As I readied myself for bed, I would imagine his approaching nearness – see him vividly returning, calling to me softly from downstairs, the mundane circuit of the kettle re-made as he set it boiling for a pot of tea. *Is that you?* On those nights I would not sleep but would feel time rushing through me and would almost hope, as though merely by its constant motion time might convey me to some other place and that way I might stand a chance of seeing him.

So I would lie there with my back to the wall, leaving empty the space for him to slip beside me. Shadows would seem to move, dissolving and re-forming in the darkened room. The house would be restless with creaks and inexplicable, silken rustles. Once I even heard the front door being opened, then quietly closed, and I swear someone entered and was standing there, an ear cocked to the luck of easy theft, although the next morning nothing had been touched. To leave the emptiness unconfronted left the chance also for dreams, and wishing things were otherwise became a habit almost of courage – or maybe it was stubbornness.

Now I can feel the circular motion of the tide beneath the boat, a gentle, mocking revolution to return me always to this one same point of unwilled continuance. I am still alive, even after all this? I can't believe it, and putting it like that I see the idiocy of whatever phrase might prop itself beside me, nerveless as a sign – for sale – outside an empty house. Because in the end there'll be no words, this much I know for sure. And whatever beginning that there once was will loop back upon itself, tail to toe, just like a dozy snake asleep in the logic of its restful body, inevitably circular.

I think now of my mother, of her canticled disguises each night, those muttered responses to a thing she couldn't fathom, though pretended to have plumbed the depths of, and could endure – as though that could ever be enough. Because my father's death transfigured her, drenching her in darkness and the humiliation of untruth: word-stupid prayer was the only lid she had to keep some cover on her sadness.

I can still see the way they were together. They'd nestle against the coat rack in the hallway where they thought I'd not notice them. They would kiss there, tight-entwined like silkworms, almost savage one against the other when he returned from sea. Then she'd come back into the room serene and laughing, the blood risen in her heat-scorched cheeks, veined with the heat of cooking and effort – and of kissing my dad. Her clothes would be slightly damp after being pressed against his sea-soaked body, and steam would rise from her when she stood with her back to the fire, drying herself out and smiling.

His return illuminated her. Her movements would all be graceful then, with a kind of smooth elegance locked about her limbs that made her lovely. Everyone who came to the house would notice it. And it's how I best remember my childhood: as though a fine thread of contentment bound us all together, drawing anyone who entered the room at the moment of my father's homecoming right into its delicate-spun net of charm. There were no words there, just as now, just as at any moment of worth throughout all life. Try to fit a word there and the moment will be damned, forever lost beneath that surrogate skin tight-plastered across true feeling.

The dusk is deepening towards an evening that bears the moon upon its surface like a precious brooch, a thing gorgeous with memories of the day's rich sunlight. But if there is only me out here, then what do these mother-memories count for? She's long dead; more dead still is my father, her husband. Still more, her own father. And are we supposed to stay steady, enduring this?

I remember seeing photographs of her father. Some formal ones with my gran, him with his hand upon her shoulder – she was straight-backed and regal in a stiff white bonnet, sitting on a thin-legged chair that made him seem enormous there beside her, kingly grand, implacable. He had eyes glittering and clever and I'd imagine him with brilliant guesswork about where to find fish. There was a picture of him in the pub, too, taken when he was very young. He was handsome and maybe still a teenager, standing in a group of grinning men, flocked about a basking shark, strung up and hanging from a makeshift gibbet on the seafront.

The picture had always made me shudder. He was a brave man, my mother would say. And I'd know she was thinking only of her husband. Though her eyes were turned towards the photograph of her father, she never fooled me, and she knew it, too. I could tell by the way she'd take my hand and press it like a leaf between her two warm palms, seeing that I was safe, remembering.

But all of this is lost, sunk now beneath time's ocean swell of tides. I pull back my hair to tie it tighter behind my head so that I can better listen to the slight remnants of sound flickering from far away, across and beneath the sea towards me, heard only through the strange siphoning motion of the boat, melodious as a conch shell, letting me know absolutely where I am – drifting about on a mass of water I can't even begin to guess at. It makes me hushed to think on the enormity of things, just to imagine the sounds and echoes of entire lives within this sea. I can dig up such great riches of remembrance just from my little aperture of listening, so then what greater depth and distance of orchestral imaginings must it bear etched into its endless layers, a constant re-making of a record of infinite incisions, liquorice darkness of sound.

I lean closer into the night, wondering how many lives the sea has listened to, and by what telepathy it must have fathomed the desires and anguish of the million sailors lost or utterly at home here. Because I could weasel my way back through just one chamber of my family's echoed past, and even then the noise of lives would be immense.

But I know it can't be done; no, there is no way of seeing other than through your own lonely eyes, your pain your own, in your own blood, unshareable. I feel the shock of knowing this, just as I knew it that childhood day my father died, as though I'd been granted a kind of unembellished prefiguring, writ small, of the massive sorrow I'd be hit with later.

Because there's nothing absolute in all of life. That's what I understood right then. Everything changes and dies. Nothing is ever caught for good. So then there's not one thing that can be held in common from one soul to another. Sure enough, there's some kind of similarity of limbs and gut-stuck exclamations that we can point to, and like a dim narcissus feel delighted to exclaim upon.

But beyond that? No. There's not a thing. We are not 'we' but only 'I', each one a little ship adrift, forever motion-troubled, not once at rest but rather flux-caught and various, shuffled about by no overseeing eye or power above or even below, but by the world itself, a brute fact hesitant and nervous, inscrutable as the sea. This is what I tell myself, gazing in silence at the perfection of water, glistening as though someone just threw saltpetre upon it –

because there's a kind of magic-trick of starlight upon the surface, since the moon's so frail it can't be casting all this light, now surely? So are the already dead stars as strong as this? Can something dead be quite so dazzling?

I am hunched against the cold, feeling the smallness of myself as a gust of ice-driven air shocks itself about my limbs, whipping me towards the littleness of whatever ending I will come to, the place where there'll be nothing more than this faint shadow to embrace. Because where are you now? I cannot call on God. No, I cannot do it. I can only call on my love who is no more here than He is. And despite whatever thousand phrases I have cloaked about me, aimed in vain to protect me from this moment, here it is – the thing that I've most dreaded, a degree of solitude beyond whatever waiting emptiness I have so far known.

Again I try to speak but there are no words here, as though what I'm after is an answer to a question only I can phrase, and yet I cannot do it, it stays unworded, as though all along it's been waiting for just this moment to present itself to me without disguises. A silent thing. Neither here nor not, caught in no particular, nor anything general. A thing that were I to attempt to write it down I'd be able to designate only by cutting a hole out of the page, just as I did with that Bible when my father died, razoring out those lies from the book so that they'd not torment me further – although they dog me still. Love. Memory. Love. Memory. Buffeting against me with the finesse of the tide, perpetual and elegant.

What else is there? I could stick my head beneath the waves and not come up for air until my brain was starved of the stuff and all this thinking and all this beauty would be lost. Because there's not a glint nor gleam of light to say another single soul upon the earth is even reckoning on it. There's only me and I'm so quickly ended, whether in fact or just by thinking that it's so. So could I do it? Could I get myself unhooked from this noose of words that's threatening to string me up like my grandpa's shark and hang me, leave me dangling like a caught thing, undangerous to me or others? Just a no-thing, then?

I see myself with that Bible blade, held in readiness. The sea is darkening about me, and I haven't yet lit any lamp aboard the boat, so there's only the moonlight and gleam of stars to see by, though in fact there's nothing whatsoever to see apart from the shiny snakeskin of the calm black water, patent and polished-seeming all around. And I wonder if it's the salt that makes this luminosity so lit with splendour. Or some kind of hidden light of all the dead souls, cavorting and mysterious beneath the surface. But this thought makes me laugh, not happily.

In my mind's eye, I have the blade ready, wondering about the incision and where to make it. My ears are open to whatever sound but there's only the falling night, making the sea quiet, untremulous, barely a single glug of it beneath the keel so that if I'm moving, certainly it's neither forwards nor back, nor even caught between those poles of motion – I am not moon-drawn any longer, my body now is a shell, no more than that; and it's as though with wondering where to make the slice to free me of myself and that way see if I'm attached to life (as once I must have been, surely that must have been the case?) I find that in fact I'm suspended as though above the surface of things, myself being just like this little carapace of boat, bobbing about upon a massive well of water.

The knife is sharp and waiting, and the only place to aim it is my heart. Sure enough, I'm just a heap of flesh and bone, I tell myself. *I* am nothing. I am only this suspended thing, dangling from a gibbet with all the life and purpose now bled out of me. I know this. I knew it the second he was gone – that there was nothing left. That I had suffered to no purpose. That the world was without sense or meaning. That life was a false thing lit up only by the illusion of love, not by any fact of the love itself. Because how can love be real if it is contained within flesh, which dies? So then nothing is real but what is now.

And yet with the night closing up my eyes, can I even be certain of what's about me? I could be anywhere, in any other night. I don't know where north or south is. My compass is all deranged and without meaning for me anyway. I didn't come to sea to navigate but to find him. And what the hell was I even thinking of, knowing that it could not be done? Why did I choose to do something I knew beforehand was impossible, set only to torment me? Maybe I've lost my mind. I say this out loud, and even grin, wondering if in fact it is the truth, that I have lost my mind through grief.

Thinking this, shifting down deeper into the arms of the boat, nestling myself into the canvas – a small wind has picked up and my limbs are hard with cold now – I am aware of something like a voice inside my head. No, I tell myself, I'll not be hearing voices. But I can't pretend it's otherwise. It's just a very little sound, not too definite at first, though gradually it's becoming so.

Is it that the sea itself can speak? Is this what's happening? I almost wonder. But no, it's not quite that, it's at the far point of all my sorrowing, some noise that's definitely human, solemn and true, reminding me of myself. It bears no articulate thought along, but is itself pure thought – just that, a quiet thought that's absolutely still, alone upon the massive ocean.

My breath stops in my throat as I hear this sound, knowing instantly what it is, a sound as lifesaving as a rope cast out for a drowner, saving them at the ultimate minute: *it's his voice and mine*, deeply bound together in my heart like the absolute purity of memory itself, a rosebud vibration of me and him together, unimaginably harmonious and lovely, so that I'm drawing back from making any kind of cut with that damaging blade which now I hold up out of harm's way, high above the sparkled surface of the great sea of memory I am floating on – *happy*, yes, that word will do to express it, sure enough – happy to my profoundest guts to have him close beside me once again. Memory, now, is more than enough.

12

Come here, he's saying, his arms a cave for me to shelter in, pressing my face against the rockish comfort of his chest, and I'll tell you what it's like at night upon the sea.

There is firelight, and it is well past summertime, with already the sun descended to make darkness of the land. We have no lights on within the house, and his face, when I tip upwards to take a peek at it, is angelic with a gleam of rosy flames upon it, brightening his blondeness to a halo. I have my fingertips within his hair, feeling my way across the smoothness of his scalp, his head shape cherished in my palms as a thing too precious, troubling me to think of. I hold my hand within his nest of hair and

Braille my way to memory of his shapes, the softness of his nape, pliable as duck down. He still bears the scent of sea upon him.

About my waist his arm entwines, drawing me closer so that he can imprint a kiss upon my brow, his lips untremulous and cool against my skin. There is the steam-borne scent of potatoes and slow-cooking vegetables from the pot on the stove, a smell of butteriness and wine-soaked delight. It is warm inside his arms, and beyond the whispering fire and the faintest hush of wind and distant tide far out beyond the rocks, there is no sound, only the descending evening.

It starts out as though you'll never be able to see anything, his voice is curious as he tells me this. I can sense the vibrations of it through his ribcage against my tight-pressed cheek as he's saying how it always makes him feel like a fool, as though there's something inadequate about people, which means they have no business to be out there on the sea at night, as though they're just not built for it and might as well pack up and go back home. The night seems final, that's the way he puts it, so that every time, it's terrifying, at least at first.

I think of it as a massive kind of harmony, he says, with the world shifting through a set of gears or notes to work its way into a different key. At first the stars seem faint and useless, pitted against the daylight still lingering within the sky which is just not dark enough to make them work. So there's a discordant not-quite night which is bothersome because it's neither one thing nor another. And it's this that brings the fear. Because it's the uncertainty that's worrying, not the thought of night.

And then suddenly, there it is, and you can sense it – a sudden rightness shot through everything, the entire scene harmonious and steady, which is the point at which the fear vanishes and you're humbled, knowing utterly your place: beneath heaven, forced to trust nature and your wits, with no pretending otherwise, or make-believing that you're something grander than you are.

He stops when he says this, his lips coming to rest again against my forehead, his voice quieter now as he continues.

And then there's nothing you can do but just be patient for the day, waiting for the fish to rise and fill the nets, be kind to you and let you snap them up and bring them home to land. Because you're far away out now, and you can't go back, the tide won't let you since you've taken that promise when you planned the trip, knowing the hours it'd take to get things square with the fish and the turn of the tide, so that you can run the whole thing together and be back at the exact right moment the sea allows you through. Too early or too late and the sea won't let you – or it'll let you but you'll have no fish and it'll be like it's spitting you back onto land in scorn since you've not taken what you came for, as though you've led her on with all your pretending, paddling and pinching about on the surface of her – and then to return without trying to take the thing you came for? No, that's not right. So the whole thing has to be harmonious, and you must trust it will be so. That's the thing to have – trust.

He's thinking I'm perhaps asleep when he tells me this. But I've heard every word. I try to keep my breath steady and shallow so he'll not hear the fear in it. Fear, as I think of him at night upon the ocean with nothing but black water and scraps of starlight all about him, no living thing upon the surface but himself, and under the surface the thousand slimy fish and God knows what else there'll be beneath. I see sea monsters when I try to think of what might lurk there. Sea monsters that'd swallow his little boat without a thought. Why shouldn't there be such things when there are so many miles of unseen depths of heaving stuff that swamps and shifts about beneath him?

So for sure there'll be monsters, and I see him whistling, his hands behind his head, his feet cocked, content, upon the transom, smiling like a child up at the stars, while behind him and with utter stealth and deviousness there's some great thing creeping closer in towards him, with rhino skin and a crust of flesh upon its burly neck like armour he'd not stand a chance with. Good God, and he's talking to me of trust, so perhaps I shiver then, because he stirs against me, stroking away the hair that's fallen across my face to lift within the currents of my breath, lifting, falling.

But there's a fear that cuts far deeper than this monstrous one, and he knows perfectly well what this fear is. He can hear it in my veins like memory with a mouth wide open and bawling at him, telling him of itself and why it will not rest. How can it? It's a fear that carries the bad blood of generations with it, solemn and persistent: the men leaving the women for the sea and not returning, leaving them to fall like cliff-dropped stones with sorrowing, stranding them on the beach where they're not even close enough to embrace as death approaches. And so how can he ask me to trust him in the face of this?

But his arms are tight around me like a promise. And I know he'd never break this faith with me if he could help it. Yet the sea is wilder now and rising up the shingle, guttering against it like a sneak of wind finding out a candle flame and licking its way against it, blasting its way towards the safety of his arms' embrace, so that soon – I know it – the light will be cut and we'll sit here in a kind of night with only my fear, and what'll he be able to do for us then?

My fingers must be hurting him because I'm clinging dogged to him now with thinking of him out there on the darkened water, without me there to share those hours stolen that I'd give my life to have, the time torn off and lost without him in it, the time that could be real if only things were otherwise. But they are not. Things are only as they are, and the sea owns half of him, will always do so, until it owns him all.

The firelight is losing strength and embered in the grating, though still it's sharp with heat. He holds me and I am temporarily safe. But I know that he can feel the fear within me, and that he knows the reasons why it's there, running hard and effortless across my skin, knifing its way through my blood even as he clasps me close and comforted against him. Hush, little one, he tells me, his breath almost silent. Calm now, no need for fear. I have the fear for us, see?

He heaves me nearer up against him, seeing that I'm still awake and listening. Do you see that that's what I can do? His voice is urgent with whispered determination. I can take the fear and hold it far away, entirely clear of us both, if you'll only let me, then all will always be well, and entirely safe. Do you see? I'll sail out to sea with it, and throw it overboard there if you like, anything so you don't have to have it. The fear can be in me, on my back, not yours, and that way we'll be safe together. Because I'll not let anything happen to me. We'll be different to your family. We'll swim against whatever tides, with a whole string of sons who'll outlive us both, and we'll be together and true until we're ancient, and I'll never let harm near you. That's how it'll be, and you only need to trust and all will be well, I promise. Come here . . .

Even though I'm nestled snug against him, that's always the way he speaks to me, wanting me only ever to get closer to him, grow ever more trusting of him, and that way, he promises, we'll be safest, as though we'll somehow forge a ring that can't be broken, a circle to be looped about us both, to keep us from all harm by that perfection, our arms the branches that will bind us there and keep us rooted.

And so that night, once more I open myself more completely to him, widely allowing him into me to plunder all that he can find. It's a particular kind of dying, the way he seems to fall down moonstruck inside me, tightly magnetised against my flesh, and powerless in the face of a vast compulsion that he must tussle with, as though stung by a harmony he's intent that I should hear, his lips gathering blood and trembling with the sound of it hot-rushed inside his veins.

Now the fire is cold within the grate, and our flesh is worn with being twined so close and nakedly. He rocks me in his arms and tells me I am safe, and for these moments I believe him. Trust is our talisman to ward off danger, and look how quick it works between us, deliberate alchemy that leaves his skin sparkled with jewels of sweat, dissolving in the hot breath of the room, and tasted away by the cat-tip of my tongue.

And even now I can make myself feel some shadowed simulacrum of that feeling of safety and fast hopefulness, even right out here on the nightbound ocean with nothing but the stars and my own small self to remember him by. Because now we re-light the fire, both of us laughing and pinkishly young, our skin stretched tight as new canvas for us to paint our secret wants upon, wrestling ourselves against the warmth of the other's flesh, bared to the firelit evening as we go in search of food, ready now and fully cooked in the finger-hot pot on the kitchen stove. So then we're lifting the lid of it, smiling at one another with the pleasure of being about to eat – my God these simple things we did that made us happy, ecstatic at the satisfaction of our own full bellies. Is it even possible we could find contentment quite so fast? Were we the luckiest pair alive, to be that easily pleased?

I'm smiling now as I remember this, the scene of me and him unbearably tender to unfold from the far part of my mind, the memory of it heating me up as though I'm right back in that lost bright room of happiness. And with my eyes shut, I can slide the sight of him through all my thoughts, silken memory of incredible luxury to see him standing once more within fingertip distance of me, turning to smile at me as I approach, his arms a loop of joy for me to step inside.

Now we're sitting together before the fire, stoked up and blazing again within the hearth. Outside, the wind has picked up and is whistling through the window frames, a fine and high-pitched sound that means the waves will be racing up the beach to the sea wall, hurrying to rush against the stones of it, making the boats restless in the harbour, and me here inside the house and glad beyond belief that he's beside me and not out there upon the horrible ocean, where if I could have my way I'd never let him go again.

The air is peppery, vivid with strings of scent to draw us towards food. The room's heat is disturbed around its edges by the wind-drawn night outside; it has crept through the casements of the windows to curl back up the chimney, circling the house with a delicate threat of weather. Rosemary, fenugreek and thyme are there inside the small room's glow of warmth, and the fire pops with pine logs bursting from their bark.

I tighten shut a curtain, taking a peek outside to see nothing there but night and the gleam of sea on stones where the waves have whipped the granite to a precious sheen of fine reflection, magnifying the magnitude of water. He has his back to me, sitting facing the fire with his arms outstretched to stab at it with a stick, whistling faintly through his teeth as though to stir a drowsy horse back to alertness. I go to him and we sit for a moment together to watch the flames grow tall, sucked up the chimney flue by the ready wind. See how everything will be fine, he tells me, as though the stoked-up fire were a magic trick of profound proof.

I can smell the faintest scent of his hair and skin, the imprints of flesh against cotton and wool. His left foot, shoeless, is resting against my ankle and he rubs against the exposed skin there, remembering himself to me. His face is avid with concentration on his bowl of steaming vegetables, hot within the dishes that are heating both our hands and making us smile at one another as we kiss before we eat, glad of food and heat like straightforward animals, with nothing in the entire world to match that bliss of fine simplicity.

But do not go imagining that by thinking on him you might make him real, I curse myself. Such a thing is just not possible. Memory spikes the flesh, merely, and once the flesh is gone there's nothing left but the emptiness that once was red with blood. How can I be breathing still when all his breath is gone? It is a damn irrelevance that I should live when everything of worth within me is hollowed out and perishing by his absence. There is no sense to life when love is lost, when all I'm capable of is a blinded stumble into ever greater darkness, knowing that whatever light I've once been guided by is utterly extinguished. Because all love dies, despite whatever hope might once have bound it up in prettiness of flesh, and love is not love when it is bound by memory alone. Then it's a diminished thing of violent cruelty and hurts, oceanic anguish that's fit only for lost drowners.

I see the last year of my life in a sudden concertina vision of airless days pressed flat together, with all the music gone and inconceivable. I see the times I could not even eat, the thought of change brought so much trouble with it. I see myself attentive only to the slide of days that stretched towards the moment I'd be free to give up hope, understanding from the start that there'd be nothing that could emulate the strange, quiet *fact* of him alive – no grief or poetry or distraction whatsoever could lament the shape that once he occupied with himself. And how I know this now, as I lie here on my back beneath the hideous beauty of the starlight that will not find him out, wherever it might chance to shine upon this unkind sea that took him from me. And how can it have done a thing like that, to leave me so alone?

13

It's an untravelled path I'm following across the night-dark ocean, and behind me the wake of broken water is dissolving faint as whorls of honey stirred in distant lifetimes. The air is sticky with fingers of salt reached off the ocean's skin to coat my face and throat in tiny fragments of the sea now glisteningly ready for me to skip inside its swollen belly, just succumb to its insistence and that way abnegate this need for choice, because what does it matter which way I turn now? A part of me is petulant with unknowing. I came out here to find him and instead have found only not-him, only more and ever greater places where he *was* and now *is not*, as though he's impressed himself across each hidden inch of sea. Now all I can do is contemplate his absence, drop lone stones inside an endless well that's without echoes, the air alive with nothing but that sound of falling.

And if I release these stones of memory? I imagine myself squatting on the edge of the well, looking down into its dark circle, into a life irretrievable, as though remembering him might be a kind of letting go – which I can't bear, since my heart's still greedy for his memory, wishing it were a thing that I could hoard and that way stash in safety from all corrosion and all change. So yes, I make a promise to myself, I will look for him at any price, even if finding him means I lose him then forever.

But I can feel him far inside me now, his voice a rhythm resonant and deep, his face as clear and distinct in my perception as though I could just lean a few inches forward and be able to taste his lips, feel his skin against my own, merely by a shift of limbs. But then in another second he's entirely gone, and then returning, moving in and out of me in solemn tides of memory that leave me cravenly wishful, wanting him near and steady. If only I could hold him, keep him close. I'm like a tightrope walker, treading the finest thread of concentration, or like a wily navigator, steering a great monster of a ship die-straight through a slender breach in the land.

Isn't this how it was throughout our lives? We lived along a fragile stem of union, our closeness the needle's eye we had to pass through to be ourselves. So now it's a stone-heavy fact, fallen and certain, that whichever way I try to think on it, he is my only way.

I look around me at the darkness, my eyes stretched wide open, as though maybe I'll catch the wisping wraith of him, slipping out of the corner of sight, the green flash of aurora borealis to light me towards true north. And as I stare, I have inside my bones the exact same urgency of waiting for him as when we first met.

I would listen for his footfall in the street, the dusty summer's mutedness of leather on stone. I know the weight of his step instantly. Even the first time he ever comes to call for me, I know it's him by the padded stealth of his big feet's pressure, slightly hesitant as though testing for quicksand. I can still hear the way he shuffles against the step for a full minute before he raises his hand to knock, and by then my mother has already come upstairs to tell me he is here, smiling and looking hard into my eyes as though to estimate the seriousness of my feeling, her face becoming tight as at the taste of lemons, not sour so much as resigned to a bitterness of worry that she knows will come to nothing.

She stands beside me where I'm caught in unreadiness, messing with over-pinned strands of hair. She lays a hand on the top of my head the way she'd do when I was very small and could still fit beneath her palm, even when I stood up to my fullest height. Now she has to reach to do it and the gesture is grave with expectation, as though it were not my life but her own being re-played, with her set back a pace from it, made to look at it from the remove of imagination. *Will it happen the same way for her?* She is plainly asking herself this when she looks at my reflection in the mirror and smiles, handing me the front-door key as she tells me not to be late, that habit of admonishment a badge to remind me only that she is my mother – meaning a thousand things, the very least of them being her request for earliness.

His hand knocking on the door makes a sound that sinks straight to my nerve ends. I can see the blood-rush to his knuckles, the pressure of skin on wood, the way he will be leaning slightly forward as though to listen for sounds of life inside the house, his face bright with wondering, his breath's quick exhalation through his nostrils, the lamplight's easy re-gilding of his dark blonde hair. The first time he's ever called for me. And I pause for a moment before going down, not through cunning, but because my heart is turned tickertape machine, clicking off each separate fact about the evening.

Lavender, fresh-cut, scents the house, voluptuous crush of purplish buds held with twine in room-corners to turn dry and grey there. The rooms are warm, the windows open to let dusk replace day with something softer than the blaze of heat that's leant upon the shore all afternoon, singeing the beach so that I half expected to see steam rise at the point where sand and water meet. The tide is low – I can hear only the far-off whisper of it hushed at the harbour mouth, licking along the lips of stone, propped open for the ocean. I am breathing through the tiny high point of my lungs which feel compressed by the swollen blood-bound longing for these seconds to span a greater stretch of life than in fact they do, as though my heartbeat, quickening, is wiser than I'll ever be, realising the urgent preciousness of each fleet moment and wanting only to match me to it, make me bigger, faster than I am, since that's the only way I'll be fit to feel one inch of the vast quantity of things that're rushing vivid and tremendous all about.

My feet make strange music on the floorboards, each plank of wood a particular key that I've known throughout my life, playing out a tune of descent as I walk across the landing to the stairs. Silvered by the half-light, the carpet glistens, ready for me to glide upon – or so it seems; my limbs become weightless but taut with wondering how it will be when at last – silly girl, and I'm lip-bitten with nerves now – I set my eyes upon him.

My legs are bare to the warmth of the evening, my feet naked in sandals soft against the skin of my toes. I smooth down the cotton of my dress and feel the heat of the flesh beneath, my blood risen to the surface of my skin as though to burst clean through it and that way meet him. It is dancing, a tiny dance with spears, all along the hidden stretches of my limbs, tickling me at my knee-backs where the hemline flips. There are few sounds beyond the constant rustle of the sea: the kitchen clock is labouring on the hour, and next door's radio sounds like birdsong. I hear him shuffle on the front doorstep, his shoes advancing, retreating, and from upstairs there's the sound of a door clicked shut and the slither of paper and cloth as my mother settles down to read.

I stand for a moment alone in the stone-flagged hallway where I can see his silhouette dark against the glass pane of the door. I breathe in as steady as my risen lungs allow, only one thought clear inside my head. *He is my only way*. For sure I have a thousand other wild imaginings all jostling about amongst the feverous fact of that one thought, but one thought is what it all amounts to – a kind of certainty that I can taste upon my lips, like an object just handed to me for verification. Yes, I'm saying, yes to whatever it is that these moments are holding ready for me. I will do whatever these new moments ask.

I press against the door, rushing at it almost as though to break it down, since I'm suddenly gripped by a flock of fears, that if I stay here much longer I'll merely get stuck in the fear of motion. So quick, go now! My mind is ordering, and then hurried forward even more by the thought, Perhaps it isn't even him, or maybe it's no one at all, perhaps no more than a loose window knocking against its frame, or even just a trick of the light. Then the worst fear of all: what if he is nothing as I know him to be? What if this time he has changed? And this is the final barb to make my limbs unsprung, propelling me forward with a show of eagerness that I do not even think to regret after, to swing open the door and find him there, my one true love absolutely there and himself, and more himself and more my love than even I had then thought possible.

Yet instead of taking a step back at the sudden fact of me burst from the house, he almost jumps forward so that we collide bang on the threshold, rocketed like magnets, inseparable – which thought is making me smile now here alone upon the sea, thinking of his stunned loveliness at that moment, having no clue whatsoever of the beauty that shone about him, much as though the lamplight from inside was emanating in fact from him, and not from some repeatable trick of electricity, so easily undone with just the faintest flick of a fingertip, a gesture entirely careless, not even liable to memory.

14

Now even God knows all about us, is what he whispers in my ear the day we walk together from the church, blessed and bound at last by marriage. He says it with a smile, his arm about my waist, his hips pressed tight against my own as we stride out into the waiting sunlight, dazzled by the day washed blue by hours of April rain.

There's orange blossom beyond the cyprus of the graveyard, and our walk is scented, the spring-time air suffused with pollen and barely even a thought of the sea that's rumbling far beneath the church, silhouetted hunk of sandstone, stuck defiant on the skyline. We're kissing beneath the gate, the space around us melodious with wishes, scattered with confetti now to land upon our heads.

We've been married forever, he's telling me, and it is entirely true: we were married in secret the moment we first met. Our eyes and hands confirmed the vow, even before we spoke. We swapped our hopes like children safe in play, confidently handing over treasured toys in sureness of receiving something more desired – ourselves, handed back tenfold and multiplied by the swift refractions of love, a prism made up of our two hearts, shining deeply one inside the other, casting massive rainbows of light that lit us up for ever after.

Our bodies embrace as close as tight-packed earth, as though no one else is near, and only when we are pushed forwards, with a delicate *Oi!* as reminder, do we think to observe the ceremony of leave-taking. Midday beams us in sunshine, and the earth is majestic, grandly solemn against the sea, which seems restful, far distant from our celebrations. The land along the clifftops is newly ploughed, ready for seeding, and the fields are fat with recent rains that must have come from clouds above the land itself – certainly the wind is smooth and offshore blowing, bearing nothing of the sea.

It's a short distance along the coastal path down to the village. On the stretch of nearby road, cars toot their horns and slow down to see us as we go, the people waving and pointing as we walk beneath the arch of silver ash trees shivering in the sunlight. The descent towards the seafront takes us past the sheep farm with the wall-eyed dog forever barking, and then down between two narrow rows of houses, a slender way, with the sea just visible at the end, its navy surface dazzlingly reflective of the midday sun high overhead. People come out of their houses to look and someone whistles at us from a sneaky upstairs window, and then vanishes. There are some early tourists too, blown here by fair weather, who stop and gawp as though our wedding were an extravagance for their pleasure, and in the harbour many boats are drawn up high, unmanned: their captains are our guests.

A buoying-up of sound and motion bears us away from the wedding party, and suddenly we are alone together in a quiet room, just him and me, and I have no notion what could ever come between us, there is no space for any other thing to fit – might as well slice apart a single body and expect it to survive as say that he and I are anything but indivisible – *he* and *love* and *I* three drawn components of an equation Gordian-tight.

We stretch out together on the sunlit bed, blank with new linen. His face is gleaming with underwater smiles, secret and desperate. I have each moment in my flesh so that the vision of me and him together will not budge from memory but lurks like an agile ghost about my body, hunkered down in secret folds of flesh, slipped in amongst sinews, and resting light and dazzling on the pin-head synapse points, ready to re-emerge and make my nerves buzz with the exactitude of memory. Because time has not brought distance, only clear-sightedness, and this fact of me and him together is not perishable with overuse but is like a fossil made apparent after years of rubbing away the stone that binds it tight within itself, revealing every second the gem of life inside, clearer, and more profound after years of undiscovery. And just so he is here right now, slow and smiling, sweet love above me, not nervous so much as like a child, innocent of anything but this, a boy as bound up in his skin and mind as I am, holding out his hand.

Fingertip to fingertip is how we nourish trust until

it's electric like creation on the ceiling of our want, with us looking up at it in wonder, the sight too beautiful, sinuous slide towards confirmation of itself, which is how it goes between us as he lifts his shirt so I can see his skin that's soft as polished marble warmed by the shine of sun-struck afternoons, smooth and matchless after weeks of heat. And there are places now that I am travelling to that can be found by no one else but me and him, small places in my soul where nothing fits but love, no words to follow after. So now our limbs lock tight, unbreakable, one inside the other, pressing close to a stencil shape precisely made so that no other shapes can match to it but ours.

I have my brow inside the shallow valley of his throat, his hands spread wide across my hips and back, with every dip and hollow of ourselves contrived to fit. We are two happy mutes, with all that is not him and me shut out so that we are islanded, complete, offering to the silent space around us this belief-shocked act of love.

His flesh is deep within me now, with nothing there between to separate and say where he is anything but me, apart from one thin veil of fast-dissolving wonder, and is it even possible that we're so close? So that with each pressure of flesh and motion, we are seeking out the door that unlocks life and heaving it wide open, clinging one to the other as ecstatic drowners might, feeling the fantastic boil of ocean trying to pull us down forever, so then our bodies down-rushing but struggling to make the fight for air worthwhile and so the fight being the thing that does in fact redeem us because here we are again, our breath profound, steadying, as we look down at last in confidence at the pearly nub of brightness we'd glimpsed together on the ocean floor, laughing at it, knowing that we'll not be drowned.

He rocks me like the water's motion, saying, There there, my love, see here we are? And I see that yes we are entirely here and now, because until this moment of re-emergence from beneath the sea of loving him I think perhaps I'd lost all sight and sanity, become instead almost an idiot with adoration of what he offers me, a kind of holiness that even now, years later and alone, leaves me skin-shocked with the joy of him and me together snug inside the other. But now I will not call on God the way that then I did. How can I bring myself to do a thing like that? My heart's so full of curses in this desolation where he *is* and *is not*, all at once – as tight-fixed inside the inner eye of my heart's best memory as he ever was, yet not beside me as he should be this very night when the sky is beautiful with stars that he'd have known all the exact names of, giving me his eyes to measure the world's loveliness by, saying, Look, there's Arcturus, which means rough weather is maybe near and imminent, so you'll be careful? And there's Capella, the goat star, and there, Corona Borealis, with Hercules still fixed and bright in struggle, and look, d'you see it, Hesperus lighting up the evening for lovestruck sailors to feel glad beneath? And then in winter, when the nights are black and the land's invisible in the darkness, over in Orion there's Rigel, the mariner's star, to see me safely home.

And this is how it is, he tells me, each evening I sail this little boat back to you. So do you understand how I navigate with no compass but constellations and my love for you to draw me back to land? Despite whatever potent tide might try to lure me seawards, still I'll find my way to you and you to me, as though we are ourselves magnetic, despite the magnetism of the moon-drawn sea that often goes against us. And you know how I always come back, he'd say, despite whatever odds?

Yes, I tell him, I know that you always do come back, so I'll trust it to be always so, and take those stars as proof.

The afternoon is stretching into a dusk that has kept the rain far distant, hunched up inside the lowering clouds now mashing on the sea's horizon, bruising one against the other, when at last we emerge from our wedding bed, the dancing long since started.

On the beach, someone plays a fiddle and a fire has been lit that shines its flames upon the thin white scuff of nuptial tide, cresting on the shoreline. The season is being kind – the rainclouds dissolve with the ending day, leaving only the faintest fuss of flies amongst the stranded seaweed – and the night is warm like embrocation on our skin, heating us up with a happiness that does not diminish but sits forever just beside us, a fiery angelic presence to keep us primed.

There's dancing on the shingled sand until rose-madder is risen from the east to match the bonfire's sparky embers, faint with sunrise. Gulls are starting already to wheel down from the nesty cliffs. Sleep-drawn, the music of voices rests lightly on the lowered tide, and threaded through this filigree of noise is his voice, which I can hear wrapped still within the whisper of the sea as it presses against the small boat's prow, nudging into tiny wavelets that surely must be wanting me to fall asleep, they are so soporific in their motion. But no, I will not sleep, how can I when he's close beside me in this night? So no, I will not do it.

And just as sailors fallen overboard are warned against the ocean's habit of sending them to sleep so death can come with delicate stealth, suffocating them in a freeze unending, when they'd been trusting the cold to be a safe salvation – so now it seems that the very second I give up on remembering, he'll be lost and me lost with him. But this is not memory and not past, this is right now – then maybe even future, since there's so much more of this for me to find, re-find and then be guided by.

So it is not memory but straightforward thought – and all the facts that rush like fire alongside thought – this fact of him beside me as he is right now within the night. And so for me to acquiesce to sleep is something I will not do because what if that's the moment when he vanishes, never to be re-found when eventually I wake? What if I wake to find he is not here?

Damn to hell my frailty, I'm cursing out loud, I must not sleep. I cannot sleep now he has come to me so close and perfect in my mind. And I am pinching myself beneath the grimy oilskin, punishing my flesh to stop this sleep from coming to devour me with jaws that are not his, pinching myself and gnashing tight my teeth, my gums soon aching with the effort of doing this absurd thing, while beneath the boat, the ocean seems to grow more slow, like a weary animal rolling idly to get up, gathering momentum with a low-slung, rocking motion, and overhead, forever lovely, the stars remind me only of my love and of all the nights he must have sat like this, his head bent skywards wondering about the chance of storms, just as I am now, this moment, with him here beside me in this little boat of memory.

I pull my right hand from its glove, and reach it out in front of me, so that it is almost dissolved in blackness since the night's so inky. And reaching it into the darkness this way, seeing its velvety disappearance into the cooling air about me, it's almost as though he's taken tight hold of my poor frail mitt and is holding it close, pressing my fingertips against his heart so I can feel the life still in him, almost fit to burst within his living chest.

15

It is the density of water that shocks me the most, my brain perhaps imagining I might turn fishlike, finding out small pockets of hidden air to breathe, effect some strange conversion of the ocean into a medium where I might live, but of course that's not the case and my skin is superfluous, no barrier at all to the impression of the sea which weighs against me heavy, ever heavier with each descending motion downwards far inside the deep that does not end.

I have my eyes stretched wide and tight within the water, hoping for nothing and finding even less than that, just a duplication of darkest matter that makes no sense. Because if all is nothing, then where's the space for nothing left to be in? There is no space, only this vast compression of miles of lead-heavy sea that now has swamped and swarmed upon me like a thousand blackened bees gone thick with anger after an absent, wanted queen. The stuff is in my eyes, rushed up my nostrils, through my ears to populate my brain with blackness, humming now along my guts and veins, arterial dash it is impossible to live through though it does not cease, so then perhaps this non-cessation is proof of continuance enough. But I am not here, how can I be? There is no space for me within this murk of fluid fullness and how I long for anything but this, some emptiness that I might breathe by, since gulping nothing would be better than this gulping up of too much stuff *and where is my love now?*

I shut my eyes and then there's something, some pale throb of colour to remind me of blood and not-sea, hot pulse in my eyelid's secret barrier against the water but it's little help, as though I'm plugging up the sea wall with an inadequate thumb already frozen stiff with helpless waiting for the sea to cease, and still the tidal push against my small defiance. But it is quieter like this, shut-eyed hope against the massive sink of salt-chock water that is slick about my limbs, impossibly frozen tub of oily stuff with pressure pressing ever further downwards, sinking me deep within itself, a sly tumble that is surely lowering me towards the ocean's bed, since doom is always downwards, never skyborne, and this thought is the only thing I have to cling to, to make sense of this at all – that I must be lodged in downwards motion, because if not that, then there's no sense whatever and that can't be so, and heaven help me if it is.

And it is now I somehow come on shafts of light, slenderest beams not quite of light so much as a delicate lessening of the dark, a mere attenuation of the blackness into something I can cling to in my mind to bring some thought of hope, though not the hope itself, still just the slightest thought of hope and some way off but that's enough to make this darkness almost well-like, a thing with walls and some dimensions, even dimensions uncertain would be better than this absolute formlessness that has until this moment mummied me in watertight shrouds of finality – and there it is again, a slight quicksilver gleam that lessens desperation, and so I cling to that, my brain brinking starvation of the thing it lives by but still, not yet, and by that separation far within the deep I have been blessed.

Darkness has fallen through the covering face of all things as though to claim them for itself and that way kill off life but now I know it has not triumphed, that there's something else besides, hovering over the face of the deep and not descending down within it but remaining sustained there, a melodious simplicity of sound perhaps, though light and breath also, so that as I fall and tumble helpless inside the thickening night of ocean I can feel the lovely calm of certainty like a faith that it will end, and ending I will be myself and that way find salvation.

Within this dream of limpid suffocation I can make out moving things – platinum flash of fishes, the choreography of dusky fins, elegant passage of massive shoals of motion that gutter and are extinguished by lowering clouds of lightlessness and the bucked up ruck of sandstorms, darkly brewed by hidden tides that rip and roll amongst the catch of seabed weed. And then the keel of limbs, tipping head over heels throughout the strenuous eddies of the sea – I see the flicker of fingertips amongst the sway of oceanic trees, the cobalt bloat of bodies and the sordid pop of eyeballs, rolling from the sockets of seafarers transfixed till death by mermaid hopes of bliss.

Something touches my toes. I do not see it but I feel the touch and my flesh seems too huge a thing to contain fear, which shrinks within my skin and patches panic across every surface of myself until I'm numb, wishing I could see the thing that reached for me, is reaching still, through the watery horror of this miles-deep murk. I feel electric with panic, and liable to shocks profound and terrifying if I can't wrest myself free of this place, which is what I'm trying desperately to do, pushing down against the water which dissolves beneath my heels. I can feel the motion upwards as a kind of stifled tightness within my throat, a sudden strangling that makes my lungs bulge and constrict with violent altercation, trying to breathe when breathing's still not possible, and now I'm flying fast and upwards through the water churning pale about my limbs, so that I'm foamed in bridal white, which means it seems entirely natural that as I push towards the surface I'm aware of the faintest pressure of his hands against my spine, a steadying caress that keeps me on an upward path towards the surface of the sea, which now I break through, able finally to breathe.

It is the absolute centre of the night, and the sky

is free of clouds so that the empty moon is wild inside its nest of stars, a dazzle of brightness all across the circle of my sight. The sea's skin is lit with moonbeams. Every inching hitch of ripple is written sharp and clear upon the water, a precision of light and darkness that offers perfect certainty. There is no sight of land. There is only the sky and stars and sea with me now cushioned soft and warm within it. I have no need of treading water to stay afloat: he has me safe within his sailor's solid hands, clasped firm about my waist, holding me there within the water as though it is not sea that has me so deliciously ensconced but his actual skin and bones sure-wrapped around me with gigantic refuge from all danger. I am afloat in him, skin-pressed against the safety of his limbs and lips as though he holds me steady from the inside out, a kind of sureness in my blood vibrating with a solemn boom that matches to the drumbeat of his heart – and just as suddenly, a letting go, and silence, absolute and terrifying.

I am canted over on my left-hand side in the bottom of the boat with my right arm wrapped about me so that my fingertips are trapped beneath the weight of my chest. The air is windless and still, the sky overhead luminously silken beneath a monstrous stretch of stars. The motion of the boat is making my stomach tip and swing like a nose-diving flight, earth-plummeting, steadying, plummeting once more. My skin feels blistered with the cold and is drenched in every pore as after a deep sea dive of many hours, wrinkling with excess of water. And in my mind's eye there is one vision only: his pinkish, fragile flesh, opalescent in the descending diminution of moonlight, falling horribly beneath the sucked tight skin of sea.

I can see his thighs braced against the slippery resistance of water, and his soft-skinned fingers clasping fleet snakes of weed that resist all purchase. His lungs breathe deep the sea that surrounds him and his veins are soon swimming with the stuff, chugging through the channels of blood to replace his life with salt-caked pipes of lifeless liquid that insinuate themselves through every part of him until there's nothing left of him to live by. My brain is hammering, full of flames with hating this, despising this futility of watching as his lovely limbs are shattering now in silence beneath the waves, dragged down ever deeper by the stone weights in his pockets.

You know there are a thousand words to mean the sea? My mother paused one day to tell me this, her eyes gone narrow to a cut of silent grey as though to warn me even then. I was just teenage when she told me, and my father had been five years dead. I remember the moment exactly, for it was lifeboat day, and each year we'd celebrate with a carnival and flags criss-crossed about the houses leading down towards the sea.

The place was noisy and the house seemed unfamiliar – full of laughter seeped in from out of doors. Her mouth tightened and I could see that she was sad to hear the frivolity of those revelries. She looked up from her book, pretended mirth, and said, Yes, there are a thousand words that represent the ocean but did you ever hear of this one – Davy Jones's locker? And she explained that no one knew quite where it came from, though for certain it was long ago, but that its casualness had long unnerved her, because it meant to say the sea was really just a tomb, implying that all those who went upon it were just dancing on the grave that soon they themselves would occupy, and surely if there's such a phrase for it you'd think the sailors would take heed now, wouldn't you, and not be quite so game to rush for death as though it were a kind of race, no more than sport?

She turned back to her reading, and I went outside to see about the day, trying not to think of all the bodies locked up – by what huge key? – beneath the secrecy of waves, harmless dish of prettiness then stretched across the sheltered bay.

Over my face now salt water has set my skin into a mask that I have not the strength to crack, as though sleep has revealed me as I am: pitted uselessly against the symmetry of my dreams and fears, which now, in waking, I can see are true, so I'll no longer fight them – though for one year to this very day I've tried, waking to a make-believe that they'd diminish but they have not, *cannot* while I'm still here to withstand them. But how I've felt this time approaching. Each morning I would wake and in my eyes there'd be encroachments of the sea itself, so there'd be no dodging of the stubborn fact of it, which would wrap itself around the house like triumph, leaving even the windows sea-encrusted with a skin of diamond salt.

Often, after nightmares, I would try to dream of leaving and of fields – but then how could I be so faithless as to turn away from something he so loved? So I'd be drawn there like a supplicant to look at it, to see if I'd discover just one meagre clue to what its sense was, and its secrets. And that way, standing there, I'd doubtless be mistaken for a person sorrowful but measured by their grief into a place of reconciliation, and not raging after all the seconds utterly then wasted while I bothered – why on earth? – to cook and eat and breathe and carry on. For what? For this?

I have that year without him like a precious piece of ice inside my skin, where even pain is better than its too-soon melting nearness. But why can't I stop my loathing for a world that made this thing a fact and not confined within the safe cage of my nightmares? Because this sea is real, and everywhere about me, and it is true that somewhere beneath this veil of darkness lies my love and could I turn fantastic diver I would dredge his body up and draw it close and tender to me, better to remember the certain fact of him that even now is stuttering, diminishing, slipping through the fingers of my brain like the foul sea that one day swallowed him entire and whole and with such vile perfection that there was not a thing left of him, not even a scrap of cloth that I might then turn sneaky fox and scent him by.

As though the sea was pure carnivorousness it chewed him up, and tickled its pretty gullet with my love's limbs until there was no fragment of him left, and I am descending into sleep again for sheer exhaustion at the stark fact of this memory, my thoughts the sullen pound against a shore of facts that will not corrode and crumble as I'd wish them to but stay instead resistant, absolute, as though the fact of my love's death were the only true one left beneath this charming waste of stars, a solemn and tormenting arch of beauty I am set to die beneath, since that way, surely, I might join him.

16

I wake to fear, a vast encircling twist of noise that fills my guts with trouble, huge vibrations of the danger of itself as though the noise and fear were interchangeable. I'm without bearings, the useless swivel of my eyes offering up no landmarks I might cling to. The blackness of the night seems deeper than before, with all the stars now vanished in a pitchy fug that makes me shiver more through fear than cold, which anyway has made my limbs mysterious, unfamiliar and impossible to shift as though I'd overnight gone waspish, drowned deep within an aspic gleam of amber many million years ago, all movement long forgotten. But this drumming trouble in my flesh won't stop, tensing like a wild crouched panther fit to pounce, a leap of noise tight close beside me, imminent and terrifying, and suddenly I realise what it is.

Inches from me, a mile high boiling wall of steel is passing by with massive swiftness – a North Sea trawler burning through the cod-starved water deadly close, the loom of bulkheads risen huge and furious with darkness blotting out all light. The wet side of the ship is silken with freight train menace, a horrendous suck of sound and hurtling speed that deafens all my screams with a finality like the stench of black-clothed terror, swift before an axe's fatal hack. On and on the wind-rushing blast of metal slices within touching distance, a giant knife's incision through the delicate skin of sea, the cut now rolling out behind within its milky wake of hurt as at last the trawler passes by, leaving nothing but liquid turmoil and the diesel reek of engine stink, evanescent on the salt-soft air.

The boat seems to gulp in breath. From beneath the keel a stunned coughing sound runs out along the hull almost as though the boat itself is shocked into a state of preparation before speech, on the brink of curses, exclamations. The back of my head is sticky and pounding, and when I unglove my hand and feel about inside the matted nest of hair, I'm touching blood from a gash that must have come from being cast over backwards against the gunwales when the boat was twisted in the trawler's wake.

There seems to be only one small light high up atop the ship, a tiny iceberg tip above its monstrous metal danger, still moving at terrible speed, entirely oblivious of my little boat that would have been swatted into nothing, had its course been set just one degree different, and I'm seized with shakes at this thought, seeing the flying wreck of splintered wood as I am suspended in a whale-spout tableau of destruction, entirely final, then descending to the sea's wide grave and deserving of no further notice as the trawler surges away along its unbent course. There's a kind of fizzing in my fingertips to think on this, and I can barely find the strength to take in air, my throat is so tight closed against the act, strangling me almost with denial at the thought of what so nearly happened.

I watch the trawler's black blot shifting away across the starlit night, leaving only memory's wound, unmatchable immensity of damage, and at last I'm gulping in air for sheer relief as much as necessity.

Something fixed has now become restless. I can almost hear the hinge of alteration swinging free. The boat is skittish as a colt afraid of snakes, and its giddy fright transmits right through the wood to me. My brain feels fast and eager, and all my thoughts are rolling forwards in surprise, still stunned by the strangeness of the now-changed night.

Yet only eyeblinks earlier, hidden in the drowning fantasy of my dream, I'd felt death like a magnet, too close and inevitable for me to draw away by any vital distance. Now my eyes are wide with night vision curiosity, seeing myself as I was just hours before, and wondering already at the steadiness of my defeat. I was prepared to give up as easily as that? Because now I have fear, as though that trawler has dredged up what scraps of life were still left in me, and as it disappears into the swallowing night I start to sense a fragile noise of hopefulness that maybe at this stage is nothing more than conscience, a bead of obligation to the deed my mind is worrying at, saying, You cannot die just yet, don't think you can, not until you've confessed everything, since your soul's not nearly pure enough and how can you have imagined that it was?

So then the surface of me is bracing itself as though

in readiness to withstand something near and dreadful that I'm sure will kill me to confront. Must I? my heart is asking. Must I face this thing I know is rumbling past me in my mind's long night, so close I think if I were to stretch my thin-skinned fingers out towards the slicing steel of memory I'd maybe draw them back to find them bloodied and close-shaven, dead by hurt.

I have my mind screwed tight against the dreadful lurking thing I know I must admit. My mind is casting curses back upon itself: Did you really think you had the power to choose your memories? Picking out only the bright-lit tops of my life's geography as though they floated there unanchored to whatever greater flush of life rushed thunderous, perpetual beneath? Because what was I thinking of, setting out to find him without a thought of all the trouble hidden just beneath the mirror of the sea? In a flash, I understand the naivety of my intent, all my courage seeming now like simple foolhardiness, imagining I could be guided only by my memory's constellations, entirely careless of the night that lay between.

But there is no starlight yet to find my bad truth out, and I am glad of that, though now I know it will be soon. As I huddle deeper down inside the boat I feel the fear wrapped all around me so I'll not escape next time. But where will I find the courage to raise my voice against this fear? I'm asking myself now. Where will I drum up the strength to be saying, Bring it on, I'll admit everything now so bring it on and still I'll live through it fine, unscathed, remembering him intact and without flaws of damage and of madness that I know I must confess? Because there is no light here whatsoever, and I'm unmade by darkness. There are no bearings left for me to reach for. There is only the looped-up skein of labyrinth thread within my mind, leading me along a path that's silver-bright with charms, fooling me towards faith, until suddenly I'm set brinking on the very last edge of the pit without even the thought of light for me to conjure by, and please God help, forgive me for the thing I now must say.

17

I am sitting in the armchair beside the window that looks out on the sea. The day is dazzling with late summer loveliness and I am smiling as I look upon it. I have a book open in my hands but for perhaps an hour or more I have not read a word: I always find it hard to concentrate when he is not on land. From where I sit, I can see the flatness of the water which appears oil-slicked and undisturbed since there's no breeze and the tide is full and not yet turning. All the other boats are back except his but still I am not worried. Even though I expected him back three hours or so ago, I am not anxious: the sea has a look benign and safe, just as I wish it'd always be – this is what I'm secretly thinking, cursing winter's storms at the same moment I'm thankful for this summer's day of peace – when I hear the sound of boots outside, collecting on the cobble.

The boots are gathering together in the street as though at a village meeting preordained that I'd not heard of. But I know it is not that.

I put my book down, very soft the gesture and entirely without haste or any sign of worry, marking the place with a ribbon fallen moments earlier from my hair and not yet put back – I'd been wrestling idly with a stubborn knot where the rubber band had held it in a heavy loop about my nape. I'd been idling there, thinking in the vaguest way about a visit to the hairdressers – Jesus Christ, was that in fact my thought at the moment when I heard those raven boots flock in the street? Yes, that idiot's humdrum thought was in truth afloat inside my mind at that moment when I heard them come. So now I'm putting down the book, letting go the noose of my hair so that it swings free and warm across my face as I stand up, smooth my hands across my skirt, pull down my sweater, straightening it across my hips, and leave the room, shutting the door behind me.

I go upstairs, my feet alone upon the over-worn

treads that need some fixing, have done for years, and that's a little thing we've said we mean to do but have not done so yet, so I make a solitary clicking sound as I go upstairs, caved momentarily inside the lightless stairwell until I come again into the light of our bedroom, where sun falls upon the white bedspread, stretched well-made and snug across the mattress.

It is here that I sit, very tidy and without unnecessary motion, upon the edge of the bed. Through the window, I can see the men outside in the street, over by the rail that runs along the seafront, before the drop onto the beach. They can't see me. There is the mist of net curtain to prevent their seeing me sitting by myself like this, watching them, knowing perfectly well from their postures and every gesture they make what has happened. It is written in their limbs. It is written there within their limbs as though each one of them was born with certain knowledge of this disaster somehow latent there inside their flesh, so that one day, even on a fine one such as this, they'd have the knowledge ready and prepared, waiting just beneath the surface of their skin so they can hand it over to whatever luckless soul was meant to hear it.

Beneath me in the street a lone car passes by and

that intrusion makes the men all turn, regroup and start to fidget with distraction, and yet still they do not come. Their feet appear meticulous, edging only further from the house and not towards it as at the commencement of a race where the start line can also mean exemption. And why do they not come yet to tell me? I have terrible wishes circling round me now, like a devil dancing near to taunt me, wishing so hard I feel my cheeks turn red, that their bad news is aimed at anyone but me. I even know the neighbour I'd intend it for and that depraved presumption makes me sicker still. Is this what danger does to us? Makes us into animals that eye with hunger carrion flesh and fight even over one another's heart's thin sinews.

I cannot stand the sight of the gathered men for a second longer, and so I turn away as though my not looking at them might postpone, or better still divert, whatever course they're set upon. Still they do not come a single pace closer. I do not hear them move. I can hear only the push of waves on up the sand and shingle, and so I count the phases of the tide, the subtle riddles around seven, rising, falling – surer cadences by far than the mechanic drag of clock-time even now pinned into dumbness on the wall downstairs, the tick tick emptying towards the truth – when there'll be no replenishment of tides to follow after.

I face the bedroom wall where there's a photograph of me and him together, and so I set my eye on that, feeling the steadiness approach, hanging there at a distance as though I'd only have to stretch my hand out and right there we'd be – something I could know by touch, and verify as surely as by senses. But there are shadows in the room, slanted duplications of the greater shadow of the cliffs which by mid-afternoon will wrap the place in darkness. Staring at that photograph, the image seems already trembling, our smiles implausible, as though inches out of frame those men outside are urgent even there, and even then are waiting with the news.

I can almost hear them as they deliver it, and I know what words they'll use: *Your husband is dead.* Garlanded with whatever flowers of regret or worry, that will be the phrase they'll utter, some moments from now but it makes no difference when. I think I heard those words long years before my birth, so that every pain I've ever known was riddled with that impeccable design of perfect sorrow. Even bruises to my childish knees reminded me of the chance of this moment almost offered to me now, and there are only a few minutes left before I'll know this doom for sure. So sitting there behind the netted-over window which rests like a cloud between the certainty of death and the almost-chance that it might not in fact be true, I am sincere in silently begging those downstairs men to linger all they like before they bring the news I know they have about them, much as though I can see them with a sack full of shoulder-hurting letters, black-bordered as with notices of fancy funerals.

But still they do not come, and part of me is saying, Look, you Goddamn fool, they have no bad news at all, you're premature and utterly ridiculous in worrying that there's any harm been done to your beloved. What an idiot you are to be worrying that harm has come to him on such a day as this when the entire sky is wonderfully blue and barely with a cloud upon it, and then beneath it there's a sea without a single sign of trouble, millpond calm, in fact, and how on earth can there be damage there today? Because remember how he left you only hours ago, at dawn? With clear and sweetest love upon his lips as you went to bring him his forgotten packed lunch, rushing after him along the street so that he turned about and, seeing it was you, pulled you close within the circle of his arms. Was that only hours ago? And him so real and living and why is it that this vision of him is already clouding over, as though soft already with long-distant memory, when it was so wonderfully recent, almost now, it was that close?

It is then that I hear the hopeless knock upon the door downstairs and I am unable to pretend for one lucky second longer that the news they bring is anything but fatal.

I know it's said a person's heart can stop and hold them free from life for great long moments at a time, as though the body comprehends far better than the mind the simple fact of anguish, new-delivered – and it is true, I feel my blood begin to lag inside my veins as though that door, just knocked, is in fact my heart too tightly held until all functions of it are suspended. I do not breathe but feel the sick rise in my throat and have to take in air to stop myself from retching.

They know I'm here, and that I have heard them. I can hear their jostles turn respectful on the doorstep as they wait for me to ready myself, go down and let them in. Yet even now I prefer delay, and I can feel whole futile minutes pass before I go downstairs.

There are five of them, unsmiling but still staring at me with a flat intent as though their looking were a float to keep me raised. One of them has been back to his house, and changed into his Sunday best. He has on a stiff and mothball-smelling jacket. I can smell it from a few feet distant, and there's a hole on the lapel where the jacket guts show through pale against the dark.

I cannot meet their eyes but fix myself upon that patch of pale and imagine the decision that he took to make that change of clothes. Yes, it will be better if I bring the news to her well-dressed, not slovenly or bearing the scent of the sea upon me, but neatly and with a formality that she'll notice and be glad of. I see him walking with an air of generous dignity back to his house, telling his wife the news before he has told me. I see the way she sits down maybe on the overstuffed arm of a horsehair chair, itching her bum to sit upon, but she'll not mind this penance for those moments of his telling her the news. Her eyes will be spilling tears perhaps – my husband was well-liked – and she will fuss within the steaming comfort of their kitchen, making tea for him, casting secret blessings skywards in thanks that he is safe and here beside her in the kitchen. Perhaps the suggestion to put that skin-scratchy suit on was hers. Yes, I imagine that perhaps it was. Do you think so, love? he would have replied to her then, accepting his wife's wisdom as the law.

So here this man is, not my husband but my husband's friend, and alongside him, jostling like lambs, an offering of assorted menfolk come to cheer him on.

They lead me, one with a hand upon my forearm – that's the suited one – into the room where a fire is lit, as though in primitive honour of the flames that mean all's well, and I feel a kind of magnetising hell-skip in my toes that seem intent on drawing me towards the fire and that way put an end to the sure news they have before it's even taken hold. Of course I do not do this. I sit down in the armchair as they bid me do, and listen as they tell me all the facts exactly as they think they must've happened.

Where were the fucking storms? I want to shout at them and that way see some sense in what they're saying – that his boat was found adrift and empty some miles westward down the coast. Someone from another village found the boat and almost wondered if there had been divers, maybe, working there and that would be the explanation for the boat's not having one soul there upon it. But no. Looking inside, they'd not found oxygen bottles, nor anything but empty nets. It seemed he had not even got that far that day. *He had not even set his nets*. And this is the thing that starts the men off twitching.

I spy one of them doing this from the corner of my eye. A youngish one, who maybe knows no manners, and has no pattern yet to fit to of quite how a man is meant to behave when there's a suspicion in his thoughts like this one. *Because what can he have been doing?* his nimble, restless feet and downturned eye and forwards angled shoulders are wondering, spelling out a question mark across the bare unspeaking facts of the case. What can he have been doing out at sea without a single net set, and so off course? He was a fisherman out in his boat clearly without a solitary intention that day of catching any fish, so then what?

I am thanking them for bringing me the news. Yes, it's thoughtful of them not to let the local bobby do it, this way there's a personal touch, which I appreciate. So I am thanking them. I am not crying. But I can tell that I am dead blue-white from the fact of someone offering rum from out his greasy pocket-stashed flask, saying, You going to be alright, love? The wife'll be over sharpish if you want her here to see you through, and shall I ask her? *Good God no!* I think I screech since he's backing off, appearing almost hurt that I don't want the meddling good intentions of his dear-heart wife to enter at any point ever into this house, and that in fact I wish these bloody men would get the hell away from here so that I can at least pretend in silence with myself that this is still our little house, with room for no one else but us, so then with room for no one *less* than us, as though the moment that they leave my love will re-emerge to fill the gap then yawning in his absence.

Yes, that's how it will be, I lie chastisingly to myself as though to wake up from a drowning dream so that any second now he'll be walking through the door. Now then, what's all this? he'll want to know, and there'll be laughter as he stands there in the doorway, golden in the late day's sunshine, with his eyes then resting kindly on my face before he comes to be alongside me with a kiss, his arms to draw me close, emphatic as the life that'll still be in him.

And I am praying hard for this absurdity, fanatical repetition within my head and silently, as they leave me to grieve with the thoughtful flask of rum left here beside me on the narrow table as they shut the door, discreet click against their disappearing backs, leaving me entirely now alone.

The house folds closed about me and I screw my eyes up tight against the sight of it so absolutely changed. Everything that's here I cannot stand and there is nothing now that I can even glance upon without a grip of horror overwhelming. Am I being buried alive? Is this what's happening, with all our relics and possessions tumbling heavy about my ears too loud with memory and the imprints of their thousand uses, all the places that our hands have jointly touched and held? The house is quiet and horrendous as a mausoleum but by God not quite, for still the sea's resilience rushes roundwards – not forwards and away but dancing on a fixity of vindication like the dance of death itself and had I just one wish that's what I'd ask for, like some lost Canute disputing why the waves should not be silent at his bidding.

I keep my eyes shut for fear of all that I will see, although I see it still as though the room has been imprinted on my retinas and will not be removed. Because it's my inner eye that sees the truth and places no false vision of him there, does not even cast a shadow of a ghost in place of the solidness of him, now gone – and he'll not come again: all my willing to discover him is gaudy as the worst illusion. The fire cracks open a new log and so the world returns and makes me look at it again.

The boat, they said, was discovered empty. And their saying this puts me straight in mind of a coffin, with his body the least and secret part of that equation, his soul already belonging to some monster far beneath the waves. I remember now how that had been the image I was struck with, seeing fangs and agile slithery creatures claiming what they could – the suddenness of it that left the little boat barely shaken on the surface of the sea, rocking as though to sleep along the score set out for it by the ocean's secret song. His death would leave the world oblivious, that much I was sure of. There'd be no marks to say his life was ever even there, and no history would shift so much as by a hair's breadth off whatever course it was already set upon. There would be no ripples and no consequence anywhere but in the tideless circuits of my blood. The boat itself would stay afloat – just as it did, just as it has, and me now here within it like his ill-formed ghost, trying to guess his moves and hear whatever echoes that he may have left.

But is that how it has to be, inevitably, in the end – the boat without a life within it? Just some shell that may or may not hold the vital flame, it makes no difference, since what's the consequence anyway of the life that's there: the boat will float without a helm. It will still bob and buck about upon the slimy ocean, whether or not a single soul's inside to guide it. And then when it's worn and all its wood is spoiled by time and too-hard trials, it will merely fall into disuse and children then will play in it for fun, rolling their eyes in imitation of bravado, with their small teeth gnashing and tremendous as they imagine pirates must be, leaping back to land for tea and scoldings.

I look about me at the beauty of the water undisturbed by all the ragings of my mind, the serenity of it not slightly nudged from off its axle-rest of fine completeness. I could hurl myself right into the world's calm eye, smash myself beyond all comprehension and there'd be no sign of it beyond the pain I'd bring to my own skull. Beauty would still be everywhere. Loveliness will outlive us all. I'll not make a scratch upon its face, and neither will a living soul alive. We'll all just pause and rage and fall, and there'll be quiet momentarily in some small corner of a body's heart, and then the lifting up again, the tide eternal pressing round about its certainty of motion – though not for us, who end.

The boat was discovered empty; they stated this so nicely, waiting for my understanding and confession: That'll be because he couldn't bear to live, not for a second longer, feeling all the things he did. And do you see that if he jumped then it was me who pushed him? Not with hands but with far stronger words – is this what you want me to tell you? Do you want to know the reason why? Is the fact of death not enough for you?

I shut my eyes and I am him again, upon my back the weight now keenly felt of everything I've tried to set aside. The loop from hearing of his death to now is drawn as tight as wire that's barbed with razored spikes of memory, so I can't unlook the visions here unveiling. Even the sea beneath is with each moment gathering, as though to try to raise me up and push me to the height of understanding that I've been too low and frail to face with anything but trembles and this worry festering wilder every eyeblink I avoid it. Because there are endings everywhere I look, finality so tightly wrapped up to inception that the whole is inconceivable to grasp from where I am: I can see only the knot of trouble, without the chance of any solution but the one that's certain for us all.

I steady myself inside the boat. The sea beneath seems swollen. The sky is darkening. The wind is now so fragile, touching my face almost with warmth, dampish, pleasant, that I can hear my own breath. My body is already grown by some degree instinctive to the sea, and its rocking motion swings me towards a state akin to calm, or certainly it's concentration as I feel the stillness of the day like kindness, or like gracious manners, even, standing smart aside to let me get a better view of a fierce race it is essential that I see: my life's the wager that's been staked. I am attentive, listening and watching out for clues of precedence.

And I wonder, did my love then also pause like

this, just for a second of ascetic contemplation of the ocean, thinking on all these things that now are wrapped about me and unshakable, however much I curse and thrash, pretending he is anything but real and here and living still, because so loved, despite whatever absence of his fragile shell of flesh. So did he stand for a second in fatal judgement on all this, the little facts of our life together, deciding they were less than nothing, signs of nothing but defeat, as his toes curled tight around the wood in wondering and careless hesitation, seeing then the monstrous inevitability of that waiting ending, magnetising him towards itself – and that way did he find it easier to step over the side of this boat which now my own body alone inhabits, and make as if to walk upon the water? Though naturally enough sinking utterly and forever beneath the sea, since he was nothing close to godlike but just a simple and imperfect, though perfectly and best beloved man.

18

There's a swell picked up and I can feel the belly rumble of the sea through the too-thin wood of the little boat's hull which trembles and vibrates as though the water is running shocks straight up towards me from the ocean's bed. Each yawling vertigo of the sea tips the boat at a terrible degree so that the propellers clutch at nothing and I doubt the boat is going anywhere at all, just heaving and whirring upon this exact same spot, so I think of angry fishes flicking tail fins up at me, as though it's this that's causing the commotion, not weather and not tides – at least until I see the first vast storm clouds, stirring up the sunrise so that the eastern sky seems embered now, and darkly smoking.

And God in hell those clouds look cruel and dangerous, and are they really storm clouds or just the last part of the night? But already I know the answer, since there's a nasty twitch now added to the water's queasy motion, making the boat skip and gutter upon the unscratched surface of the sea as though to dig a loophole through it and pull the woven threads apart so that the wooden dish and me within it can just rat-slip through the hole and find a place to sink.

There is too little wind to make sense of the swell. The waves are not wind-driven but weirdly moon-pulled, and the water is absolutely smooth, as though the surface of it has been ironed by a tremendous pressure, invisible heaviness in the air, while the colour of it is shifting every second, a fleet-flying patchwork of a thousand shades of black.

It's not the sea that will ever get me – he would often use this phrase, not smiling as he said it, his eyes averted. And help me now but I am seeing what he meant. Because it is not sea that now surrounds me half so much as all the things the sea can do. For what's the sea but a giant heap of wet? So no, I'll not just call it sea, but everything under the sun that speaks of death and trouble inhuman that can't be stopped or ever set against, so that if there were a way to catch the fear that makes a person mad, afraid to live, the fear would look like this – the ever-changing ocean, various, invincible.

I turn the engine off – it serves no purpose, its blades still windmilling into air – and scramble up to see about the little foresail, seldom used except in times like this. I've seen them raise such sails a thousand times but the ropes are oily and impossible in my hands. There is no rain but already I'm sodden to my skin: each time the boat slips down a shiny wave face, the wave beneath is broken, sending up sudden splats of frozen water which find their way right down my neck and soon are coursing in the once-warm air pocket between my flesh and clothes. I take my gloves off to get a better grip on the sail as it uncurls from the place it's stowed, tight and neat, exactly as he last made it. And my God how can I not be broken up like the fist-crush of petals just to have done this thing? Am I stone to not go wild with the impossibility of ever again seeing evidence of his labour, of his life?

The sail slaps to starboard with a crack, not full of wind at first but merely snapped there by the giddy motion of the boat, so I make it secure and clamber back to the stern to take the helm, peeking at the blackening sky and wondering if the storm will shift still closer. I try to feign wise guesswork but in truth I've not the first clue what the weather's doing, and so I just hunker down and wait, steadying myself with an outstretched arm against the transom.

There's a small breeze strengthening every second so that soon the sail is grown fat with wind, and each time we dip down into the troughs of sea, I can feel the welcome tug of motion forwards from the small sail's power, tending me up out of the darkening pits with a sudden tug each time I fall. And every moment, sure enough, the breeze is growing sharper until now there's no point calling it by that name since I might as well face the fact that this is the wingtip of some mammoth wind-born thing, its power apparent in each gust of air which seems to bear the unfamiliarity of changing scents upon it, muddy ice and the brackish tang of weed prised from the ocean's bed.

The surface of the water is wrinkled now that the wind is petulant upon it, shifting twitchily and cross as though its only constancy is constant change. There are colours here that I've not dreamt of, and now I'm right-angled to the swell as the boat dives downwards, the sea-guts opening up for me to take a closer look inside, the surface of the heaved-up wave as dark as freshly founded iron, until suddenly, as the boat shoots skywards, there's the purest shade of ink-blue bright azure at its high point where the transparency of its tip lets through the light. And no one but me will ever see this sight again, because already everything I'm sure of – only this, everything that is right now – is transformed in less than an eyeblink, so that my mind is click-clacking off like a terrible switch to override each instinct I might have left in me towards rational thought, saying, Let go, don't cling to sanity or anything that pretends to certainty because you'll not find him there but somewhere hidden within this place right now where logic's lost and useless.

My hand is aching with hanging on to the tiller's thrash and it's harder every second now to see beyond the nearest wave. Am I going to die this way? I ask myself, with not the slightest slick of remorse left for the life I might be leaving, and my teeth are ridiculously grin-bared just to think on this, the salt spume dashed against my bitten lips and running through my gums. *Come on then, see what you can do!* I lean back hard against the boat, fixed and ready for whatever the sea might have in store, though tipping my eyes heavenwards my heart is jumping fierce against my ribcage to see how fast the clouds have gathered. There seems to be no end to them, as though the whole sky has just been inked, a botched job done with hasty blotting and bruising too, though not yet rent by cuts of lightning, which is what I fear, since beneath the roar of water I can hear a growling animally rough and strong, though still far distant – a kind of thunder nothing like the fragile landbound stuff I'm used to but full of echoes as from caverns measureless and monstrous, and how deep do they say the sea can be? I've heard tell of depths to do with Empire States stacked thousand upon thousand, and say that can't be so because how can any soul alive then know what creeps within such depths?

There's a tilting lake of water gathered in the hull and I watch it slop there, and does this mean a rock has cracked against the wood and sprung a hole? Please no, that's not a way I'd like to die, not slowly, but if I must then with a sudden blackness absolute, so that I notice nothing of the nearby fact of it until it's done and I am merely dead, not knowing of it, just entirely ended then.

Now the lowering sky is yellowish and sick-seeming in a way I know is not the start of sunrise but the storm's deep-gilded eye, deceptive tunnel of trouble that leads only to more sky, brought ever closer on the back of the starting lightning, great bolts of static danger from the north.

My mouth and nose and ears are full of sea so that there is no difference between myself and the wetness that surrounds me and I'm turned incompetently fishlike, with the stuff I'm swimming in itself also slippery as the underbelly of a jumping herring that's tricky to get hold of and utterly lovely to admire just for itself. So even in the thick of it, I'm welking out the calmest vein of wonder, with my eyes as wide as the stinging saltiness allows, thinking, How is it possible that the world can do this? Just look at it! And thinking this unveils for me a kind of natural deep-struck trust in the shock of what's around me that at last I can feel, as though for one entire year of his being gone I've not had the faculty for appreciation of anything beyond the emptiness that lurked and sat like mute annihilation in my heart, saying all things end right here in absolutely nothing, just an empty place where once was life. But now this weltering crash of stuff pounding louder and more drummish all about and at last I can feel something again, and even if it's the something that squats on the brink of chaos, at least it's *something* and there's nothing I can do but be entirely sure of that one fact.

But it's the second I feel this slender rope of almost-trust that the darkness starts to come again, fear-borne on the ocean's breast, a dart of nerve-bound trouble to remind me that I'll not find calm, since there are things I'm not admitting and my soul is far from cleansed by this grand show of absolution, far from it. And so again I am cursing what God there ever was and damning his heart to hell, because it feels like a practical fact of casual significance that I've no hope whatsoever of living through this thunder, as though the water itself brimmed over with the loudness of the sound that's brought each part of itself to the boil so that the boat appears to steam and strain against the cracking wildness of the sky's black roar, and where on earth can I hide now? For pity's sake, give me somewhere to hide where I can avoid confession of this thornish thing that's stuck inside me.

My thighs are squared hard and stiff against the swollen wood and I have a rope wrapped round my arms and blistering the skin beneath my jacket, ripping through the flesh each time the sea dashes me beneath another frenzied wave of sound and motion. And I spy on the language of prayer as from a massive distance, deriding it absolutely since there is no way to catch one jot of what is happening here now that the world is lit with lightning so close overhead the sky is blinding, locust-thick with cuts of light – nothing left but water, light and noise and darkness, with somewhere in my guts a thing emerging like a monster from the muddied ocean floor; a truth I'd hoped to hide from but it's impossible that I should.

I'm on my back and drenched with water even then, years back in my memory's fragile silver on the day my son was born – and there the words are pushed out from my mind at last. *My son*, and I have tried and failed for years to keep myself from ever even dreaming he was true, though how I know it now, can feel the fact of parturition in my flesh more elemental than whatever this fierce day can hurl upon me. Did I really think evasion of this fact would remain possible at whatever final reckoning I was brought to? Forgetting is falling from me so I'm reeling at the tyranny it must've taken to pretend he did not happen, astonished to glimpse what blasphemy I wrote so stupidly across the world in lieu of facing up to truth.

The boy enters the world on a river of blood and water. He shoots from the bows of my body with a violence that leaves me half dead, unable to have further children after, so that the speed of his birth and the fact of its finality rockets me into the shock of devotion, saving me in that fierce instant from the riddled patterns of myself. See, I'm not trapped in *I*, the one who loses love, but am reborn as *we*, the three of us a skein of certainty and hope cast out into the future, looping right around us from the past to link us up in love.

His skin is lucid with a beauty that I cannot phrase. It slips from me the moment I try to snare it, even to myself with hidden words of desperate poetry. And this fact of silence seems to me to be salvation from all danger. Because something so pure and innocent, such a fact of love, incarnate, cannot perish or come to any kind of harm, how could it? For that would mean the world is hell, and of course it is not so. It is a good place where faith can often happen.

And by this eager logic my mind soon tricks me into a state of trust and happy unreflection that later almost makes me mad, since soon enough I see that life is no more than an idiot's frangible hankering after a sense to things when there is none, not one drop of it for pity anywhere beneath the gaping mouth of heaven, though certainly I was fool enough for near on a lifetime to imagine that this was not so – that we had by our trinity of steady love somehow put a stop to every pattern preordained long years before my birth, as though love could ever make sufficient difference to unhinge whatever desperate history it tried to set itself against.

But of course it can't. The storm-rent sea is a broken mouth of anger gnashed and furious, scragging my matchstick boat of memory in its teeth in perfect proof of everything now lifting from my guts in hateful recognition. Of course love cannot shift a life forever off what axis it once was stuck on, of course love cannot move these savage mountains of the sea, and so it's wise to hope for nothing and be content, flat-passive in the face of all inevitability and never swim against whatever tide your life's been caught in.

But this fact, naturally, I discover far too late, since by that time our son is dead, murdered by the sea.

19

They look like funeral pyres ablaze upon the noonday tide, three more boats being burnt for no reason anyone here can put a name to without chasing after it with a curse. The sun is nothing but a blot of colour low in the winter sky, a flat unrefraction of the brighter flames beneath, so that the sea-skin seems to be torn, an open wound, from boat to shore. There's a crowd gathered along the harbour wall, a hunk of men and women setting themselves apart with rigid hate against the suited fellow with his clipboard and his mudless car, waiting at the water's edge to see that they've carried out his command: three more boats to be burnt. It's an order from on high that says it must be so, and so be it.

The flames are not yet dead and in the sea's wide grave when already the man is firing up his car, reversing – can he not feel the union burst of willpower, wishing him to tip into the sea? And he comes perilously close, with the water so full and thunderous, drawn right up over the beach to blanket the sand with a massive weight of thrashing and intent that seems to me to be set upon one thing: to crush the land and all who meddle there.

The women now are floating like black ash smuts up into the village, leaving the men to gather closer round and lumpishly, setting their shoulders against the sight of the sea and of their boats, burning still upon it. There is a wind picked up across the water, drawing itself more tightly over the swollen tide and there must have been storms far out there, beyond the mist-hidden horizon – either that, or storms soon coming.

I watch the scene from behind the glass of the kitchen window, salt-crusted with the dust-fine debris of last week's gales. The sea is witness to the weather. It is murky with it even now, remembering the profound stirring and silting up of the ocean's bed that makes it thick as river water that bears the breaking of its banks within it. There's been enough driftwood, this last week, to build a house – so I heard someone say – and the beach has been alive with scavengers, tugging at the sea's bleached deliveries, the weird contorted boughs and buckled planks fresh from the hulls of broken boats.

Now lean rain obscures the brightness of the flames, though it doesn't douse them out, and the trinity of bonfires sits like courage in the driven mist. I cannot hear the men from here but from the fact they do not budge I can tell their curses and their fat disgust, stubborn marks of defiance in their eagle-hunched bodies that will not fall into forgetfulness or acceptance of this sight. Something will come of this indignity, and it's foolish to imagine otherwise, their turned backs tell me. This is our damn patch of sea and there'll always be new generations bursting eager with the need to fish it. They're mad to think this is not so.

And I swear the sea is growing heavier every moment, so that now the burning boats flash in and out of sight, strange lighthouses set too close to the harbour's edge, already beyond all peril. And into this weather, bare minutes from now, my son will soon be sailing. I have made a promise to him and he'll not let me break it now, weather or no. There is no purpose in my standing here, hating the sea. He is close behind me, his arm reaching out to rest across my shoulder's peak, the mountain of his mother long since scaled: eighteen, he is almost full-grown and already taller than his father, though not by much, perhaps a tiny inch which they enjoy to fight about, wanting to be big and outgrown of each other, begging me to be the final arbiter, although I'll not be drawn to referee upon their silliness. Because there's no pretending otherwise: the son outgrew his father some time back, and both know this is true.

It's not so bad as it looks, is the expression I have heard a thousand times and still don't understand. It looks as though there'll be a storm, and so there will be – that is bad enough for me. It is midwinter, just past the cusp of January, and so for sure there'll be a storm, or maybe ten of them stacked up, the proud sea's booty, rich and ready.

But I have made my promise: think of anything you would rather do than go to sea and I'll support you – this is how it goes, the hope I'd tried to bribe my son with – and if you've thought of nothing by your eighteenth birthday, then I'll let you go to sea, and not before. Your father will be the one to take you and you'll do all he says, or there'll be trouble. This is my promise to our son who stands beside me now, his hand testing out the mood of his mother and finding her resigned, compliant. He is already dressed for the sea, his slender body wrapped against the weather.

He turned eighteen this morning, at six o'clock. He woke early and I could hear him humming to himself downstairs as he made us tea, hoping, I suppose, to lessen the blow he knew I'd feel at that foul thought of him hopping aboard his father's boat and setting out in this bad weather. Oh, but you're a silly one, he's chuckling at me now. There's thousands that go out to sea and so few harmed. And you'll not give me your blessings? There is no malice in his crossness, only a slip of wonder that I'll dare tempt fate by letting him leave home without well wishes. So I turn from my view of the rain-stabbed sea, the sky pitchy with malcontent, scuffed up even in the harbour where the water's most protected by the granite lumps that break the tide in two. I turn from this to look upon my seabound son and see within his face the exact same look of certainty and longing that his father wears perpetually, wrapped like sanctified cloth of gold about his brows. He grins at me, putting his big hands upon my shoulders and gripping me there, pinned at arm's length as though to root me to some spot of certainty that I cannot feel.

You're a silly one, he says again, still smiling at me, tipping his father's blondeness from his eyes as he looks down. He is barely needing to shave and yet look at his mad itch to be a man, and if only I could keep him here and safe but what mother can ever do that to her child? I have to let him break free from me and so I smile back at him and he takes this as some kind of sign, since he's saying, Ah now, that's better, Mum, isn't it? See, I'll be fine. I'm fully grown, look at me!

But when I look at him I see nothing but my child, helpless pink-skinned boy. I see the way his baby legs kicked and thrashed in delight the day he was baptised, loving the water even then as though that font was a tiny sea for him to play in. He's a proper little fish, the vicar had laughed to see him happy to be splashed, the way he giggled with his eyes wide open as the water fell upon his head. But what's he thinking of to be heading out into the rocky sea, its boulder smash a thing inevitable? God protect you, is all I say, which makes him frown, laughing at me as though I must be dim to ask for such deliverance.

I don't need God, I'm alright as I am, he tells me close up to my ear, his arms wrapped right about me in a way that unnerves me still: when did he grow to have such massive arms? Where's the fingertip touch that could barely reach round my neck when he used to cling there, struggled against my breast, and does he think since he's a man that he'll be safe?

We hold each other that way, with him telling me how he'll be fine and happy and what adventures he'll have out there, the stuff he'll see that he'll report on and won't that be grand, for me to hear the things he'll do? And I want to ask him if he has the slightest clue how many men have been before him, and will he be exempt from all their troubles? But I am biting back this thought so that in seconds I'll be able to smile up at him as he goes striding off towards whatever future he might choose to furrow for himself, I'll be able to smile at him and wish him well.

No, I'll not stand in the way of whatever life he wants to make for himself, of course I'll not do any such thing as that. But please make sure it is a life he's able to discover, and let there not be endings out there for my boy to be unmade upon but only new beginnings, a stretch of life without unnatural end.

There are no words to fit about my prayer but it has something of this in it – a plea for blessings on my son, and with one eye upon the world outside, I find that even now I'm smiling at him as he fastens up his coat and makes some exclamation on the time. See, the weather's already turning nice, he tells me. And there is some truth in what he says, the sky becoming mottled with faint clots of clouds that are paling all the darkness of the storm. There's even an illumination from the sun, a kind of haloing of the hump-backed line of far horizon, and it could be just my wishing it but the sea itself seems glassier in the minutes that we've stood here and discussed it. See! He's laughing. Fair weather favours fine sailors, and look over there! He takes my shoulder and leans with me towards the window, pointing out the hardening burst of colour from a starting rainbow, cutting north to south across the sky.

So it is with smiles and a forward-tilting of his shoulders that he leaves the house. He sets his back to me as he goes seawards down the street, his footsteps purposeful with dignity, and when he returns that evening, just beyond the start of dark, there is a fixity about his limbs that blankets out his boyhood.

The day he died, the noonday sun turned black, and there was no light at all until the next day came. It was the same time of year, though many years later, as that first time he ever went to sea. He was thirty-three, and not yet married: his sweetheart would not quite relent, although he begged her, so she promised to do it soon, and was regretful of her delay ever after, or so she said, swearing to God that she'd have done it, had she known. But God or no God, it makes no difference either way. Our son is gone. I have no power to make it otherwise.

20

I am on my knees and in the darkness but I cannot pray. I have neither nerve nor spirit left for prayer within me and looking hard inside I can find nothing there but hatred. What kind of a world is it to have done this thing to us, taking from us the only son we ever had, the only child that I was ever capable of?

Beneath my breath I have sharp curses rushing fast and sinuous across the edges of my brain now thin with trouble, seeing no difference between the facts, implacable, and all this horrid well of mad-loose feeling rumbling ever louder alongside. There is no sense in anything living upon the earth. There is no sense to it when death comes with such importance and yet no consequence beyond an absolute and solemn end to things. For where's the point to any ceremony or sorrow when all life's ended thus? I damn the world and everything that lives within it, and fast upon damnation comes the shock: *I can no longer love.*

My husband's feet are soft upon the stairs so I can barely hear him coming through the house. But I have no need. I know how things will be forever after. I do not need more signals of his sorrow. And I have no need of the sight of him to understand the way that he will be. We are both dead already, since I have lost this spring of love within my heart. I see it all now, the future flat with certainty of worry and unchange, with no hope of new life there to add dimension.

I am envious of *things*. The sight of physical objects clustered all about me fills my thoughts with dread. They are too permanent, too inscrutable with secret fingerprints of our son that I will never even guess at. And their permanence is torment, as though they've gathered themselves up and found a place in time where they can stop, be steady and compact, like remnants of an action of great certainty and force, when I have none.

As I hear his gentle pad grow nearer on the landing,

this one fact seems implacable and true: that all affection is no more than memory, a kind of honeyed sentiment to sticky up each moment with the next one, just a way of linking up life's blinks of joy. And it is a false way, too, I tell myself, with nothing sure between to bind each moment, only the little instants of happiness raised up from the flood of nothing-stuff, oceanic darkness that's unknowable as ghosts and just as senseless – no more than a phantom of life, always shadowing after the facts, which are right now, this sunken verity of our son's death already swallowed by the seconds running after. Because we should be wearing scars upon our skin, remembering this, I tell myself. And likewise, a smaller voice is wondering still, what about the stack of happiness? Where is it now? I cannot even get a glimpse of it.

I hang my head, no longer trying to pray but merely sightless in the dark, hearing my husband hesitate outside the door in a way he's never done before. Always, in the past, he'd dash through doorways; it was his habit to do so, as though he could not bear to hesitate but had to rush across the myriad thresholds of his life before they vanished. And he would always enter rooms smiling, looking for me. But that can't happen now. No more of that. I feel the certainty of this new death-in-life as surely as though it were a thing of lead, hung heavy and perpetual about my stubborn neck – because I'll not relent. I cannot do this simple thing. I cannot look across the slight horizon of the nearing seconds and say, There lies life, there, see it there? There, too, is some point to things, some chance or likelihood of hope. I cannot do this because I cannot feel that this is true. The facts already say enough. The boy is dead. And damn those who insist that good will triumph, that hatred comes to nothing. Love comes to nothing, and that's the greater truth.

He stands within the doorframe, looking down at where I'm buckled by the bed, tipped over on my knees like a finished machine, with all the electric usefulness of me wiped out and done with. I look over at him. There is light in the room now that he has opened the door upon the daytime. His body wears a halo of luminous familiarity but the soul within him's gone, deep-buried beneath his grief and my blindness, and still I cannot move one inch to shift towards him, even to offer comfort.

They found the body of our son – though those

that found it said it could have been a thousand others, it was so hideous with the anger of the sea, black-blue as though it'd been dipped in cheap ink that had flooded through him and written him over with the memory of his killing. They knew him by his teeth – that's what they told us – and by the little talisman he wore about his neck, a tiny silver cross we'd given him at birth. It had his name upon it, and still does now, as it lies there far beneath the heavy earth they tipped down on his coffin. The way it thrummed upon the oak and brass made bile rise in my throat: that sound should be for those who've lived a longer life, death-rattling out the last chords of their breath as though to say farewell. It's not a sound for children, or for any that have not gone reconciled to earth.

My husband is a man now ancient-looking, almost strange. It happened swifter than any recognition, and even his voice is faint, incurious, needful of a love I cannot give. He says my name only, and holds his hand towards me so that I can stand up off the stupid floor where I am refusing still to pray but locked here in a hatred that I know appals him. He sees me. He sees the loathing in my face, and I know that he is noticing for the first time an ugliness in me, the fact that despair has broken the seal on whatever beauty I was wrapped in only because he loved me and I loved him. And now I cannot feel it. Either his love or my own, or anything at all, as though all feeling has been sponged away by the vast attraction of this sorrow.

But his hand is still held out towards me and his back is stiff, as though his body felt ashamed of my confessed humiliation, the brokenness apparent in my every limb, I shouldn't wonder, though I couldn't care a damn for the way I look, not now. His hand is still outstretched and I do not take it, so he leans towards me and presses it against my shoulder which is risen inches up above itself, vulture-hunched with abandonment, fixed against whatever further trouble there'll be lurking here – and I'm sure there will be more.

I feel his touch as from another life, as though he were a different man entirely, and me a different woman. I turn my head slightly, angling it so I can see his hand upon me, the lovely size and weight of it a thing remembered so faint and distantly that I can barely think how we were ever near, beloved. And is it true? My heart goes panic-jumping to think that this is so. His fingers grip against my flesh and he is shaking me very slightly as though to rouse me from deep sleep, saying my name, C'mon now, can you hear me? Each word a book pressed close upon another so that there's a library of longing in his invocation, though still I do not budge and feel the countless walls between us that I'll not break down.

We are separate, unreachable to each other and I was an idiot ever to think otherwise, is the way my mind is going, shutting itself up with a kind of glee that is a form of evil, saying, No, you'll not find comfort here and don't pretend you ever will.

My hand slips up fast without my intending it and comes to rest on his although I do not cry. We are still in funeral black and it is barely hours since we left our dead son in that graveyard. Our skin is still frozen with waiting beside the hole that took him. My shoes still bear the red earth's mud.

Perhaps he falls, or at least crumples down to crouch beside me like a nervous cat, the two of us almost fighting as I grapple him against me, my fingernails' dig against his skin unnoticed within the gasping anguish of his tears that are making his chest cave in upon itself as though I'd kicked him there with massive boots of damage. He is tiny as a child inside my arms and yet I feel no pity, and please forgive me for the fact that I have nothing now to give, though what kind of a person am I to be failing him now? So still I have him tussled tight against me with all thoughts born of trouble now and not of love.

The door has swung closed behind him and we are couched on a bed of darkness, barely able to make out anything of each other beyond the glassy well of one another's eyes as we keel over, as though this lightlessness were a drowning for us all, pressing us towards the pit where no life is. I take his head in my hands and hold it there so I can better tell him how our lives must be. That there is one way only for us to shift beyond this black place where we are and that is silence. We must never talk of our son's death. We must live from now as though we'd never had him. It is too great a grief and so we must not speak of it. This will be our pact, a promise that we both must make or else we'll go clean mad with it, wallowing and sorrowing as though it could make the slightest bit of difference.

He leans away from me as though I'd drawn a knife at him and raises up his arms to ward me off. His lips are parted and his breath is rushing through the circuits of his throat and lungs so that his chest seems swollen, strained with effort. His fingertips twitch, scratching, pressing at the air, and he arches his back as though struggling to bend back in time, to jolt his blood into an earlier flow that he could tolerate. And then he makes a noise that is no word at all, unwilled, unnoticed, and his face goes still, relenting: he is a different man, transformed within a stretch of unseen seconds somewhere far inside that he and I can only guess at.

Will you do this thing for me? I take his cheekbones tight between my palms, hating the tender shape of him that I can marvel at as though he were an admired painting, not my love. His eyes are black balls of glass there in the private darkness. He has them wide-stretched at me despite the tears that flood fast down his face in torrents I could drink from.

Do you know what you're saying? His arms hang futile at his side. He has no power left for any embracing. Do you know what you are asking of me? His voice is steady, despite his tears, and I can feel him leaving me, drawing away from me, seeing how I am failing him. Yes, I know what I am asking but it's all there is for us to do – to make-believe life is not so.

He takes my hands away from his face and stands up very quietly, no longer crying. He does not hesitate as he leaves the room but I can feel his eyes imprinting me upon them – not the woman I now am, but the one I was before I pushed him from my heart.

Morning is still beyond the horizon, with the storm-smashed sea like marcasites darkly glistening in a wettish crack of light, constantly shifting towards a greater glitter. The boat skids and falters, caught up in the hidden conflict of the undertow forever running furious in opposition to the surface hush of wind. Each time the boat drops, it seems to list more than the time before, pitching with the weariness of a drunk. Water rises vertically from the crests of waves, scatters like grain cast across noisy glass. My chest is sore with crying and I have no tears left. I have my hands entwined, one inside the other and only when I look at them clutched together do I see the attitude that they've jumped into, urgent praying for my soul in absolute sincerity.

And I feel the plain brightness of confession rushing through me now so zephyrous and sure. Because I blamed him for my son's death, and in the back rooms of my heart I hated him for ever giving me a child, still more for tempting him the way I thought he must've done, away towards the sea. And had I the chance to shuffle back the pack of days, I'd aim for that one first of all, try to create the whole thing over in some other way and then – perhaps? – the days that followed after might have passed along a different course.

Had I the chance – my God the wishfulness of generations set there like a fine brocade to elevate the frailty of the moment. *Had I* at ten thousand points across my life done different things to what I in fact did, *then* . . . But I did not, and time is captured in a noose of grammar – *had I, then . . . but* . . . The whole world's worry ending there?

No. The room was quiet when he left it. There was nothing sensible in our grief. I traced the passage of his footsteps on their route downstairs and then outside into the street. He stayed away for hours. First light had just broken by the time he returned. He did not come to bed. I heard him sit downstairs, still dressed in mourning, in front of the fire that'd long since embered. There I found him when it was properly daytime, and he did not meet my eye.

We were polite, unmade not just by the fact of our son's death but by ourselves, as though we'd stepped together into those parts of maps entirely without landmarks – such places still exist – that have written across them *No Known Settlements Here*. Or as though we'd been handed a sea chart and told that by its weird configurations we had to guess at what was set on land. We could not do it. Every attempt ended in confusion.

I watch my hands still struggling with each other as though curved about the smooth necessity of an egg, incubating change. My throat lets little breath pass through. I am sick with too much time spent wishing. I have our lost life heavily about me. I am transfixed here by it still, just the same way as I was on that very first day of turning from him. We did not live. We did not seem to rest or be restless, but were suspended impotent alongside one another, amazed at the distances that cannot be breached, when the journey travelled is not travelled willingly.

Our manners and affection towards one another

were entirely gracious, and immeasurably kind. But it was the kindness of dancing ghosts, wraith-like suffering in the limits of our toes, that secretly were bloodied, festering with a penitent's sores. We moved about the house like people entranced by a vow, not freely taken. Death sat lightly between us, and yet its levity was decisive.

Had I been different at that moment – I see us together again in the finished bedroom, on our knees beside the bed, my hands flowering his sweet face in preciousness, so dearly missed it makes my skin grow raw again with nerves. I see us together, and the vision shudders now so slightly, like a rusted train departing, moving one wheel's revolution from me so that I can look at it, and wonder, and regret but almost calmly now, or if not calmly, then with a feeling nearly wise, perhaps.

And it's as though these weighted thoughts of blame are now unlocked and link by link becoming looser, then unclasped, impartial as a chain of word-bound facts that I can spy on from the lighter place of memory, distanced from the shadow of myself by time.

In my lungs the breath grows steady and full.

There's blood returning to my limbs and dancing through my body. My lips are sore and cracking with the novelty of near smiles. The boat beneath feels benign, the sea tremendous, barely able to be fatal and no more a tomb than a soft cradle that might nudge me equally to life.

I look about me. There is nothing upon the water, no sign of any other living thing. There's only the new day's opening burst of loveliness that I am seeing now with something more than eyes, as though the beauty of the scene is magnified, bearing me with it, so that the sea and sky and sun reflected on the water are vibrating with a greater light source that I feel within my skin.

And is it possible for someone to be so reckless with their life as me? Because it is only in these moments that I recognise what I have done, the extent of self-inflicted hell that I have volunteered to leap into – a chasm set between myself and life. Could I have been so dangerous as to think that by our silence and my hatred I could cast a spell to charm away my poor son's death? I'm stunned to think that this is what I tried to do, as though I'd taken up a willing blindfold to muffle up my heart and that way try to kid myself the world was never brightly here and lit with massive bolts of suddenness and fortune waiting only to be seen – although this is precisely what I did that day I shut my eyes to love, pretending it could make no difference. Forever damn whatever weakness made me so foolish as to do that. I am smiling as I curse aloud, a fierce smile like a mile-high skydiver returned at last to earth, when all the truth I'll ever need is here and everywhere in everything I can see.

21

I swear it's true that storms have eyes – certainly one disgusting cyclops eye to sink inside, a jelly swamp of too-close sight that can't be understood until the space of afterwards. Because I have no way of telling how long I lived inside the storm, yet now that it is over, it's impossible to comprehend that it was ever real. I half expect to see the back of it – a tail flick of clouds and scaly sea, or hear an echo's screeching suck of air, fast evacuation of noise across the ocean's surface. But there is nothing, and its end is as final as a body's last blink.

I can hear dripping, and the fragile mewling of a wing-torn gull. Beyond this: just a shell of infinite beauty oystered all around, with the sky now trembling limpid in the early start of dawn.

The boat is still full of shakes and reeling slightly like a steeplechaser steaming with new triumph, its soaked, expanded flanks made taut with effort. Horizon-bound, the sun is veiled in distant mist but the sky above, and in the west, is entirely empty, absolutely clean of clouds. I am on my back beneath it, nerveless with exhaustion. Certainly I have slept but I have no idea at what point I must have fallen there. My skin feels sodden after hours of drenching, and so I wrestle myself out of my oilskin, unpeel the lanolin-greasy sweater beneath, and hang them out to dry across the bows.

Each second the sky is growing stronger, opalescent pallor soon strengthening into blue, with the sun shot wild with mustard beams of colour that I feel bound to, as though the boat were drawn towards that far-off blot of life. I have my breath in my ears and the sound is a steady comfort of continuance, the only thing to link me to anything that's gone before. Because there is no sign of either threat or damage in the sea. It reflects the early sky with a pinkish gleam like a fat trout's belly and reveals nothing of its recent mess of danger that I can barely believe I've lived beyond, sure that some part of me must have stopped back then within the storm.

My limbs stretched out like damp rags drying in the sunshine are entirely unfamiliar. I'd been certain they'd bear the storm's harsh paw marks, my body ribboned into strangeness by night-time attacks. But there's not much damage done, apart from the lacerations round my wrists where the rope chaffed, and a graze against the side of my face that I can't see but which bloodies my fingers when I discover it, holding up my hands to wonder at the red sight of the stuff, the most certain colour I can see beyond the tremulous variations of sea-sky blue, set now against the rising yellow of the sun.

I am afraid to turn round and look behind, as though I've been cannoned straight out of a tunnel of threats, a place of utter darkness, so that to look back will mean I'm sucked once more beneath the gristled eye of chaos. Even the boat seems to be lighter upon the water, tiptoeing across the subtle rucking drum of waves that bears no sign of the storm upon its surface, remembering it only deep within its guts, its groans all hidden by the thin skin of apparent calm.

But I'm through the eye and seeing clearly now:

our son's face waking fiercely tear-splashed in the dead of night, the way he'd be so quick to comfort and would chuckle back to sleep so that we'd laugh, muffled laughter, at the sweetness of his scrunched up toes as they uncurled themselves to soporific bliss. He would sleep so easily and long, flat on his back right through his boyhood, in almost the exact same posture as when he was first-born. We'd often spy on him at night, amazed at his contentment, the way he'd have his hands raised towards his head as though he'd been sleeping in the sun for hours, growing that way plantishly in the dark as though it were sunlight. He was little for years, but when he grew it was a kind of defiance at his days of being small, and each week he'd seem to be stretching beyond the limits of his clothes, growing so fast that he'd complain of pains inside his bones and people would joke with him about racks, and him being stuck on them by his parents in the sneak of night.

When he was very small, he'd often whisper to us through the darkness when he'd been scared by dreams. We'd hear him talking to us down the corridor, fixed in his bed by a bravery that he relented on by holding conversations with us as though we were beside him, chattering away like a little bee content with humming distant from his hive. Shall we call to him? we'd debate, and sometimes go to fetch him, let him in our room where he would insist he'd be no trouble and would curl up like a happy cat across our feet, purring almost with relief, no longer talking against his dreams. He said he often dreamed of being at sea, and it was true his fascination for the water was a thing we could not quench. The two of us would go each day to meet his father if he returned while it was light, and he'd prance ahead of me along the harbour wall while he was still far distant, pointing and yelping out at the approaching boat as though it was miraculous to him that his dad came back.

Only later, when he was a teenager, did he confess to me how all his childhood nightmares had been entirely made of this: his father, drowning in the night. He said he came to sleep upon our bed not to find comfort for himself, but to make sure his father's feet were safely rooted to the land, and not dabbling with the sea, kicking without purchase, as though he thought he was a kind of anchor to fix his father upon a spot where he could keep him safe, and how I envied him that neat simplicity of logic.

I shut my eyes against the blue that's without limits, needful now of nothing but the brightness of these visions fixed as compass points to guide me through the troubles of my heart, guideless labyrinth of anguish that I have fought against for years. And surely I've been recovered by a voodoo charm from the worst kind of possession: heartsick suffering that saw no end but only more and deeper darkness. Because until these gifts of plain remembrance, I'd not been able to dredge up from my mind a single memory of our son that was not black with grieving, and now here he is again as bright and lovely as though he in fact lived and could be touched and looked upon exactly as he was.

I can feel the sunlight against my flesh, and the breeze that flows within it is almost warm. The sea trips prettily beneath the waking day, gathering itself in idle, silken bolts of ruffled motion, entirely harmless-seeming with a coquette's simplicity of intent, cajoling with the promise of skin's nuzzled revelation.

The water is chuckling once more beneath the keel, a lightly laughing sound like our son's nocturnal giggle, as though he's prodding at me gently from beneath the sea, laying down his child's full-trustful body to anchor me in safety, saying, C'mon Ma, no need for your worrying after me, I'll be fine. So that I can remember precisely how we'd walk up to the hilltop as lookouts for his dad, and he'd tell me stories about how it would be when he was old enough to join him. He'd reach up his arm and put it on my shoulder, chattering away until we reached the clifftop where he'd flatten himself in the meadowgrass and sit for hours with his binoculars, spying on the cobles as they came in, naming each one and pretending to divine what luck they'd had by how far sunk each boat was in the water.

There he is! He'd start waving long before it was even possible anyone could see him flapping about there, although his dad would later swear he could see the boy from miles out. Then we'd be back down to the village to see them come in from the harbour wall, him striding ahead of me now, whistling and telling me to hurry, no need then for my shoulder's comfort.

Even in midwinter he'd insist we went up there to watch from on the clifftop. Or if it was very dark, or impossible to be out because of snow or storms, he'd set up indoors vigil in the attic room that had the best view of the sea. I'd call up for him from downstairs and often have to go up there to bring him down. Sometimes I'd take him mugs of hot milk and find him sitting there wrapped in blankets, polishing the window with steamy breath and a cuff to get a clearer view. He'd always grin to see me, saying, Any minute now. He'll be back soon, don't worry, his eyes sparkled and confident, for my sake only. Because I'd catch him sometimes when the seas were bad, sitting up there with homework or a book, pretending he was doing anything but look out for his dad, as though his return was effortless, a thing that had no need of his anticipation. It would happen, whether he looked for him or no.

But it was a kind of superstition, he admitted to me years later. Caring too much could cause trouble, he said, and so by pretending to himself that he wasn't anxious, his dad would come home sooner. If I show how big my fear is, he said, who knows how bad things might turn out?

But his dad always returned home for him. So in his eyes, his superstitious tricks worked, and his faith had some foundation. See, I'm always proved right, he'd laugh, skipping downstairs once he'd seen the boat snug berthed back in the harbour, and he'd be scavenging for food in the kitchen to munch upon while he went outside to help bring in the catch. I'd watch him go then, and think to myself, yes, he's right to have such trust, as though the boy was clear-sighted in his faith, and all my worry was only the myopia of age, muddying everything in doubt.

There is no sign of land, nor of any other boat upon the water, just the new day's sunrise shedding light across the sea, and I can almost not believe I've been afloat for one day only. I feel as though I've spent my whole life here, as though memory, at last cut open with this storm-born blade of truth, has peeled away the dross of fear and too-hard mental fight – that in the end meant merely anguish, a brain-trouble that nearly brought me down for good – to diamond-set the only things of worth within my heart. I can number them, hold them steady now, as though I've at last got them fixed in the sights of a telescopic glass that has rediscovered a long-dead constellation, fiercely luminous though lost from every memory but my own. The sight is dazzling to my eyes, and I have to shut them tight to hide the bright blue sky above me so I can see these stars without distraction: they are my life.

22

Into my eyes fine rain is falling, and all across the surface of the sea there's a delicate mist just risen and suspended momentarily like earth-drawn absolution. The boat is nudging sideways to the swell, tipping slightly as the tide turns it about, and I know what this must mean: I am somewhere close to land, though there's nothing visible yet but water and the violet light of dawn, strengthening to blue, as the sun steers entirely clear now of the sea's horizon.

Remembering last night's storm, the ocean is still swollen, yawling far beneath. But the surface of it is quiet, tickled by raindrops which each second are growing heavier, so that the sea has become a vast instrument, this little boat the thing that plucks upon its harpish strings, making it melodious. A thousand brights of light are here – none that I have seen until this moment, every one a wordless gift of wonder, angelic-seeming in the start of day. And have I in fact been blind? I feel as though some skin has sloughed from off my eyes; but even then, it is much more than that: I have been soul-blind. And it makes me shake, my bones tremulous and unquiet, to think how long this vast black thing has weighed about me.

I sit straight-backed in the boat, nervous even to budge an inch, as though by moving either left or right I might cast off this loveliness that I am cloaked in. To move from this spot would be sheer recklessness, I'm sure of it. So I sit tight and try to see what's here, as though merely by looking I might tattoo my inner eye with Lilliput versions of the scene that's massively about me. I don't want to miss a thing, my brain is chattering away behind me, clocking up gradations of colour and light as though it's never known such stuff before, ticking off and storing everything about this morning as though it were the very first, with memory the only light to guide me through from this day to the next – that thought landing like shock inside my mind. *I am going to live*. I had not intended to do so: those cans of diesel were not for fuel but fire.

And suddenly he is again beside me, as though by seeing the way the whole world fits together, harmonious rhythm of sense and perception, it's entirely natural for him to re-emerge and claim his place within it. Without him, things would still be out of joint, illogical, with a pit of emptiness razored out from the tight-woven cloth of life then liable to unravelling. So of course he's still here, I'm grinning as I see the ready truth of this, of course he is. How could I have been so faithless as to think otherwise? I'm still here, then so is he, entwined as ever in all that's most myself, persistent thread of life I've not let go of, despite my best attempts to come unbound from it.

So with one hand raised against the brightness of the sun, I have my eyes fixed limpet-like upon the sea, not daring now to move in case by turning round I see the space which otherwise could be filled by him. Motionless, I can't say for a fact that he's not here: I know he's here as surely as though he were in fact sitting right next to me, his hips clipping mine as he shifts his position to turn more closely to me, saying

There you are, now you're my girl again. I can see you now and that way watch over you too, and that's better, isn't it? His arms tightening their embrace as he tells me with his heart how he knows I didn't mean him harm by blaming him for our son's death, and that his forgiveness was always mine, I had only to look upon it and I'd see. But I have been soul-blind, and I turned from love. I know this now as though it were a fact that has clothed me all my life, so tight I've barely given it account – that redemption means only that you open wide your heart to love, and how have I been so stupid as to forget this?

I shut my eyes, feeling the water start to pour down from the sky to drench me absolutely. His arms are wrapped around me and I can feel his mouth against my face, running warm and close across my cheekbones and towards my lips, covering me in kisses, desperately missed. He has his face buried in the slope of my neck and I can smell his skin and hair, damp with hours of rain exactly as he is the day we get caught in it one time out walking on the moors. I have the day precisely in me, re-making me as I remember it.

We're tipping down the side of Devil's Cauldron,

falling on our bums to slip down yards of scree and well-sprung heather – it's early autumn and the heather is richly purple – and suddenly he disappears from sight. Seconds later, I discover why, and fall inside the same sheep's nook that he has landed in, hidden by a yellow blaze of gorse. Our jaws are aching after hours of laughter and we are sopping with the warm rain that's been falling now for hours so that we are mud-covered and exhausted after setting our shoulders against the weight of it, circumnavigating the rim of this massive out-scooped space in the earth where Ice Age flows have casually passed through, creating a huge soft hollow for us to kiss in.

Now we're embraced and lurking like muddy bog people beneath the meagre shelter of the gorse, watching the rain grow heavier, with us fixed in the thick of it, right under the clouds' rumbled passage across the land. He has his lips against my throat and we are bellyful of laughter at the beauty of the day which has us so neatly in its hands, reminding us what it can do and childing us that way, making us feel glad and small. We lie for hours there, kissing and talking, chewing on damp sweets until the rain is dissolved by a solid intervention of sunlight that makes the heather steam as we stride out through it to find our bikes and home.

And later that day, our skin still warm after the heat of an Epsom-salted bath – our limbs are ragged with effort so we can barely walk straight, we are so wobbled by that hike – we fall to bed exhausted, waking only once the sun is down, with a dusky half-light making shadows of our skin, as though we are only ghostily entwined, somewhere secret even from ourselves, hidden maybe in the balmy sap of sleep, so that weeks later his face opens wide with the utter seriousness of pleasure, stunned to learn that that night I conceived our son. Was it after the storm? he asks, as though I've performed a magic trick he's never even heard of. Was it then and are you sure? Yes, I tell him. It was then and I am absolutely sure of everything.

The rain is spearing through the surface of the sea as though to harpoon monstrous fish, leaping off the water in fierce bright blades of silver. And I am glad at this thought of knives, as though the weather itself were cutting through the skin that's kept me from the world, showing me I'm no different, that I'm likewise liable to transformations, subject to both storms and sun. Because I had come to think I was already dead, seeing my life in a vast flat pitch of monumental fixity, susceptible to no revolution. And is there a greater error a person can ever make than that? To say, there, I'm done, my life is over. I have gone astray, so now blackness sits like an already-lived future in my mind, and ever after there'll be no change and no surprises, nothing new for me upon the earth, no chance of luck or even life.

But now I have my eyes wide open, taking in as much of the world as I can fit there. And as I stare, hungry for the stuff that's here all free about me, it's as though my inner eye is restful now, seeing everything in its right perspective, finely balanced between light and dark, held steady and vibrating with a harmony I cannot fight. I am so certain of his presence here beside me that at last I'm able to breathe in peace, realising when I do that for the entire black year of him being gone I have not relished one single breath that kept me living, but resented each second I was alive without him. And at last I've found you, I say to myself, uncertain then whether it is my voice or in fact his, whispered on the tide.

The rainclouds now have gone from overhead. I can see the darkened water turn to silver once they've passed, and there's a gathering wind drummed up and bearing with it the final warmth of summer. Although I can't yet see the land, I can smell the faintest facts of it – slight scents of earth and grass. And even now I can see him smiling and calm, lovelier and more precious each second as he tells me that there's not a single cause for fear, not any longer, that he has me safe and in his loved embrace, so that I swear I can feel his hands upon my skin, holding me warm against him, his fingers' soft caress against my throat and clutching sweet about my shoulders, so that every muscle in my body seems to be expanding with relief immeasurable, almost like the relief of death that's after massive weights of pain. But now I know it is not death he's leading me towards but life, turning me round to fix my back against the black night of my soul, denying it all licence so that it merely dissolves behind me, shivering heavenwards, becoming absolutely powerless to touch the greater brightness of the light.

I have his hand in mine and I'm content, certain of everything and calm in that certainty, wondering only how close I am to land. The morning is quickening into life, and when I look about me now it appears almost precisely the way it did one year ago to the exact same day, when he went out to sea, did not return. But how was it then, really? a voice very quiet and curious is asking. Although I've thought on this a thousand times, all my imaginings have been lost within the depth of missing him. Because what was it like for him, setting out, alone, to die? *My only love, how on earth must it have been?*

I'm asking this question almost ear-cocked as though in hope of an answer – though you know all there is to know, my mind is chiding me, leave off asking more than you are needful of, accept things as they are, and do not head along whatever lightless path your fear is getting fixed on.

So I sit there indecisive for a moment, as though contemplating a black box set out of reach upon a cupboard's top. I watch the way the dark thing seems to hover, just beyond my fingers' grasp, and I'm torn, part of me urging myself to live with whatever sorrow lies concealed there, the other part saying, no, not yet, you've still to look upon his hurt before you're able to be free of it. And all this while, he's sitting silently beside me, motionless and watchful, without clues. I'll just not be true to myself until I take a closer look, is some kind of decision, and once taken, I am marvelling at it, remembering how only yesterday I'd steeled myself for leaving with that exact same thought, aiming out to sea with only one intention: to find him again, bring him back home to my heart. I'll not be true to myself otherwise – this thought like a whip's crack, distantly conceived, so that I'm once more bracing myself against whatever danger now may come.

23

He can hear the sea's fat yawn of trouble, disguised by the high-tide tickle of waves against rock, even before he has set his eyes upon it. Often, he finds himself wondering if the sound of the sea has not imprinted itself somehow on the delicate drum of his inner ear, pincushioning the flesh with hidden marks of memory, like an oversung recitative that drugs the brain into forgetfulness, so that only when he hears the sea itself – as now he does, rounding the building-backs onto the harbour wall – does he realise how poor a copy is his fear. And here he stops, his feet faltering on cobble, as he thinks on this, that *sea* and *fear* are entirely interchangeable in the secret nocturnes of his heart.

Of course, he confesses none of this to me. Instead he talks of everything he loves about the monstrous, shifting beast of water that each day he goes to ride upon. He tells me silly tales of wily fish, uncatchable and clever, the way they flock together and only sheepishly are caught. He describes the moonshine glitter of herrings, net-snared and hauled up to the surface towards fishermen's gloats, and the way that at the point of nightfall there is little that's more lovely than that platinum flash of fish.

But it's the *fact* of fear that troubles him more than he'll ever confess – either to me, or to himself – the fact of it waiting in every shifting inch of sea, which is perhaps the worst part of it: the second he has the fear fixed, it's changed, protean mass of worry that he cannot name or catch; he can only dance about upon its surface in his foolish boat, trawling up small proofs of his almost-bravery, and hauling them back on land like a prize that in his heart he knows has no significance when set against the mess of trouble that he's been wondering on all day, stuck out there alone.

I can see, with perfect clarity, the way he left the last time, his arm raised briefly in farewell, then falling to his side like a pennant torn down by the wind.

Sometimes, when there is no moon and he's alone upon the water with no sight of any other boat at all but only the faintest blink of light from off the land, tiny evidence of the world he's left behind, he looks inside himself and is stunned at the void that's opening there – a little cage of unspoken hurt that he can't wrest free of. And he looks about him at the absurd monstrosity of beauty and unseen terror, and is struck by the sudden looseness he feels at moments such as this, the way all life is entirely re-routeable, its axis utterly susceptible to change, just by one minute sliver of action, the choice to do one thing or another.

He has no answer to this worry. He averts his eyes from where it squats, shoulder-bunched, ill-omened. He rests his gaze instead upon the land and mimics the behaviour of a man who's wise enough to see some purpose to his suffering, to the sore and heavy weight he bears of his son's death. Because certainly, he thinks to himself, I can see no purpose in this pain.

I can imagine him clearly now: he has his fingertips resting lightly upon the humming wood of the boat, shaking with the engine's coughed-out exertion homewards, away from the sea and the lurking stuff within it, and he rolls the word *homewards* around his mouth like an ambiguous wine, before gulping it down and releasing more fuel to the motor, thinking, with a smile, At least you're wired up to the right route home because if you should slip now, then what?

He has the entire and terrible blackness of the ocean, its circular motions of tidal hell, fixed always at his back, and before him only the on-off switch of possible life that's left for him on shore. So with the fear at his back he is racing homewards, his heart a maniac's worry against his ribcage, smashing itself absurdly there as he pits the boat against the ocean, terrified that it will be at this moment of fright that trouble comes – a pit or trough of water, sudden squall or bluster that would capsize his tiny boat and send him down to a doom entirely of his manufacture, as though just thinking of the absolute constancy of nothingness might bring annihilation closer.

His homewards journey is always a prayer: Thank God for my life on land, and please God let me return to it, these two terrors so closely intertwined that they are indivisible in his heart, which then beats faster, so that only once he's back inside the circle of my arms can he find calm, reassured by the fact of me and him entwined, with all his fear confined again to dreams.

But it is the variation of the thing that bothers him the most. Just when he thinks he has caught it by the tail to scrogg it and destroy it, there it is again, and often smiling with the feline calm of summertime, just as it is today.

He still has the sound of my footsteps in his ears as he clears the buttress of the cliffs and feels the North Sea scoop the boat up in its palm and hold it there with a threat that is invisible: looking at the sea from the land, you'd never think today held any danger. Both sea and sky are blue, perfect mirrors of one another, with neither darkness nor clouds anywhere upon them. But there must have been a storm in some other country, because the memory of it is inside the ocean's core, and it is grumbling still with anger at this upset. He talks to the water as though it were an unpredictable pet, liable to uncompliance. Come on, he says to it, you don't want to be anything but sweet to me today, now do you? And he looks ahead to see where he will set his nets.

The surface of the water is undulant, unblown by any breeze that might make its mark upon the glassiness of it, so that leaning over the side, he can even see himself reflected there, a hunk of yellow like a sunken sun, glistening against the water that at this moment seems to have nothing at all within it, only more of itself, and he sees that he'll have to go further down the coast today to stand in any hope of snaring fish. He shifts his course a touch more westwards, away from the lifting sun, now raised a fraction clearer of the sea.

But still he has my footsteps in his ears, and he sends mental thanks up to the weather for being so kind towards him. Because what did she want to come running after me in the street for? It has unnerved him, the fact that I could be so reckless of the superstition that forbids such things, rushing after him the way I did – and just to bring his lunch. But he puts this worry from his mind and smiles instead at the brazen calm of the day ahead, no trouble here that he can see.

Yet there are hours that gape between his certainty and fear, and soon enough the fear twists restless around the keel, making the boat tremble and grow skittish. He knows the reason for my confidence, and still it makes no difference to his sense of incremental trouble, the tides now gathering and bothersome beneath, as they prepare themselves for turning. I am confident, and almost entirely happy, because for the first time in almost five years of our son being dead, I have seen an ending to our separation.

It is the night before he leaves and we are beneath a thin sheet, not needing anything but that: the air is heavy with late summer's heat and even the open window admits no cooler breeze. An hour or so has passed since we have said goodnight, though neither of us sleeps. And he could almost be talking to himself, he bites on the words and seems to chew them back, even as they tip out from his mouth. I'm just so tired, my love, is all he says. But I hear the plea snug down inside his voice, and though I've heard him make a similar invocation so many times since our son died, still, I have not heard the fact of it until right now.

The room itself appears almost to sigh. Neither of us moves. He makes no other sound, as though that phrase was drawn out from the far part of his lungs, using up the last, most precious bit of breath. I imagine his body deflated, at the limits of all effort, waiting for a sign to live again. He does not speak.

His silence, I can tell, means tears, and I know that his face will be steeled against them as they roll into the rough fleece of his hair. For him, tears are an icecap's melting, no kind of outpouring but the unstemmed erosion of a massive depth of hard-felt trouble. Still, he does not take breath.

Low tide makes the night outside sound reverent with quiet. The cliffs' bulked curvature around the village is emptied even of the water's whispers, held in abeyance beyond the harbour wall: everything is caught up in the poise of silence, momentarily.

And so I turn to him and him to me and we embrace in tentative admission of the distance travelled from ourselves, and from each other. I'm just so tired, my love, he's saying over in my ears, and I miss us. Where've we been? It's not *us* to be so far apart, now is it?

Resistance is fragile and we crush it into obsolescence, leave no space for it between us. That's better, he says, his mouth warm against my eyelids as though to guard against the chance of tears, although it's a confession, too: his tears are the ones I'm lapping from the angle of his brow-bone, the concave delicacy of his throat.

Matched together, our bodies seem far cleverer than whatever instinct our minds have had us trust, and in the shadows of the room I can feel him smiling as we're separated only by a fine skin of salt water gathering between us as we sleep entwined. I have his head in my hands and he presses it urgently there, pulling my arms more tightly about him, my fingertips held within kissing distance of his lips, our toes wriggling together like gloves.

We have not slept like this for many months but have lain there like monastic twins practising for their blithe graves in solemn abstinence from life. Now the heat is again between us, and the fear of death because it would mean parting. Which is why by morning I was sure I'd caught the tail of hope, had found it snared there in that hinge of phrase – I'm just so tired, my love – and so I'm reckless of all superstition, running out after him in the street with his tin-foiled bag of sandwiches. My God, and was someone watching and malicious at that moment, seeing the burst of optimism that I felt then?

So he's drawn westwards in search of fish and following the pathway of the sun, while I am back on land, feeling the lack of him as never before, missing him in every patch of flesh and bone, longing for him to get back safe on land so we can begin again. Because look at the time we've wasted, I want to tell him, and have I really left you in any doubt about how much I am dipped in love for you?

Now there's still no wind to speak of, and he's lolled against the prow, leaning over to take a view upon the water, and deliberating that way he spies himself again within the darkness. The sight makes him start back, and he curses himself for ever looking. The glimpse of himself there, all wreathed in black, is sufficient funeral reminder of things he'd rather, please, forget, and so in a moment he can feel the fear again, its tugging chuck against the boat as though the nasty thing was taunting him with outstretched paws, scratching against the thin-skinned boat, liable to leaks.

He sits back hard against the wood and swears some more but for all his swearing he cannot shift his fear, which floats about him as reminder. He squints up at the sun – nothing there to make him doubt or worry. And within view, there's still the land, somnolent band of calm being brought to life by morning's rosy glow.

But it is not this that causes him his trouble. It is the thing itself, the ever-waiting noonday darkness that he has sat upon for years, foolish with defiance. And here it is, he's thinking to himself, the fever thought that starts to rush and make him want to run fast from himself because he cannot stop and fight.

I know exactly how he will look at this moment. His right hand will be pressed and kneading against the middle of his brow as though to pressure into malleability the iron-stuck things that lurk there. He'll be thinking about the night before but looking back at it like a bookend to the months that lay behind, and he'll have the blame scored there within him. She's right. I should never have let our son go out to sea that day he died – if ever – but certainly not that day. She was entirely right to say the storms were fatal and how then could I think to allow such a thing?

He'll have this blame fixed like a written curse upon his forehead, marking him forever for disaster, as though it were inevitable, and my telling him it was so was just a noticing of a fact that anyone with eyes could see. But it wasn't your fault, I want to yell at him. The fault is mine in blaming you, not yours in not being able to divine the weather. Because how could you have stopped the sea from leaping up and drowning him? It was the sea itself that did this thing. It was not you.

But still he sits there, shoulder-hunched with the conviction of guilt. I want to shout out at this vision of him now guttering towards the lightlessness of endings, and can I not slide back in time to stop what's going to happen?

Because he's standing up now, unsteady aboard the wave-tipped boat, the sun hot and fierce above him, raised towards the high masthead of a noon that he'll not live beyond. And please let some power on earth allow me back there to change what's just beyond these seconds of his fear. He is opening wide his eyes and underneath his breath he's saying, *Sorry, sorry*, to himself and me, the sound expelled from out his lungs as little more than a request for silence, going *shhhh* to mingle with the sea.

He lowers his hand from his forehead and I can hear him trying to steady his breathing. He notices a dark-winged gull high overhead, fleet across the dazzle of the sun, and he thinks to himself how that will be the last living thing he ever sees, and he is smiling as he thinks this, although his smile is a sign of all the hatred that at this moment is about to swamp him as he thinks about the day that our son died – and the fact that he was almost casual when he said to him, It's rough out today, are you sure you should be going? Of course, he also tried to insist *but not enough* that he stayed on shore, using himself as example: he did not go out to fish that day but stayed in the harbour and, with one eye on our unreturning son, fixed his nets.

But I was not firm enough, is now the way he thinks upon that day, even though he was in fact angry at the boy, telling him he was an idiot to put the thought of money above his life, because wasn't that what he was doing, by risking himself for an unpaid debt? But Dad, I'll be fine, what're you mothering me for? I'm a full-grown man and you can't watch over me forever. C'mon, you're shaming me in front of the lads, and will you stop it?

This is what he is remembering now as he stands there in the gentle boat a mile or so out from shore, his nets not yet set, the engine off. He stands up on the gunwale, steadying himself as he crouches there, peering over into the sea, crossing himself with the other hand, his last thought, She's right to blame me for his death. It was my fault and so an eye for an eye, a life for a life, and what's mine worth when it's so laden full of guilt?

I can see him standing there alone, only briefly hesitant, telling himself his death is merely an inevitability and that it's courage that has brought it sooner. Because it's too late for us now to be reconciled. It's just too late – this thought the last one and already swamped as he slips with little noise into the sea, which overwhelms him, drawing him deep inside itself, borne down as he is by the dumb weight of his pocketed stones.

24

The breath is gusting from me and I am struggling for air, my eyes screwed tight against the thought of my love's last seconds. I can almost hear the echoes of the splash he made just then, his toes skywards to speed up his descent into the sea. My limbs feel light and unfamiliar, and holding out my hand I'm seeing it with eyes that aren't my own, each moment of his last day relived, repeated now exactly as it happened.

This day could have been pressed from the precise same mould as the day he left, and looking about me I know my powerlessness even more than ever, the world seeming to me to be a machine set up to run along a design I cannot help but follow, my part in it pre-set to a relentless tick-tock of bad blood unquenchable, with the world all sleek about me, leaving me no other path but this: *to be as he was*. Because there's only one space left for me to fit inside this scene of gathering and needful purpose, and that is the one that he's left empty by his suicide. I am dressed in his clothes, thinking with his thoughts, wondering only how he was that day, and is there anything about me left to fight against this natural magnetism of the earth? The earth has seized me. I can do nothing now but follow where it leads.

And there's great comfort here to think that I am him. I am certain of how things must go, and that certainty flows over my skin like honey, sweetening all fear until I find myself smiling as I look upon the ocean's pitchy slew of water, tipped and smooth beneath the ascending sun.

Yes, this is exactly how the day would have begun, just this way, the scene entirely harmless-looking, though he'd know better, understanding perfectly that trouble is patient, dogged and adept at waiting for the precise moment when it can slip its spike beneath the largest ball of calm, and tip it that way, with minimum effort, clean off its axis.

So I see him standing here inside the boat, moments from his death, with one hand raised to press against his forehead as though to quieten down the nag that's there within his thoughts. Why live with this great pain when here's the reason for all worry, waiting, offering me an ending to this knot of trouble-love that's otherwise forever in me? I have his coat about me like an armoury of courage, looking out to sea with eyes I've borrowed for so long now they've become my sole inheritance of a life of loving him. Just eyes to spy upon this emptiness with.

I can see how his hand is raised, but when I look more closely I see that it is not clutching at his forehead as I'd thought, but pointing away from the light that's rising ever faster and with a speed that's visible, aloof from the blank horizon. Each degree of greater light also makes the scene grow clearer. The sea itself is given definition. No longer does it seem to be a swamping, singular mass of obscure change and motion, but as the daylight strengthens, dispelling mist, instead the sea appears to be composed of intricate threads of light and colour jostling and interlinking, each separate-seeming part resting in fact upon another, an infinite concoction, necessarily entwined.

He has his back to the light and is pointing towards a sheen of colour that I think might be the land. He turns to me so that the sun half falls across his face, which is not torn with worry as I'd thought, but actually smiling as he points at the little band of grey – not much more than a wisp of smoky ambiguity, so faint it could almost be low cloud, although already it is strengthening into something greenish, and yes, definitely land. Look, he points, do you see it?

And so I follow where his finger is aimed and then I see it, barely visible but definitely so, which is why I stand up now to get a better look, his hand again upon my shoulder, keeping me steady and afloat upon the silty sea.

Look, he's saying, you can just see the clifftops above the village. Do you see them? And do you remember how we'd go up there to kip for hours when it was fine, treating that meadow like a massive bed for us to doze upon, and do you remember the way we'd do that, even when we weren't so young? And think on all those afternoons we'd go there with our son and you'd have him tied to you on reins for fear he'd tumble off the edge, and he'd arch his little back at first in protest but soon enough be happy to be tied to you that way, tugging on his lead like a naughty animal to wake you up if you were tired.

It is true. These things are jewelled in my memory, deeply shining there with a worn lustre made more gorgeous by the darkness they are set in. And look now at the village – he is turning to me to smile as he points at the land, the place where our whole life happened. Look how it sparks and is all neat inside the sunlight, precious and set tight in the red earth of the cliff face, and can you believe that's where we live? And of course – and now he draws me closer to him – up there on the high point of the coastline, do you see it? The church where we first met and then were married. Do you see it, that tiny blot of sandstone set against the trees?

His hand is a gentle weight across my shoulders beneath my hair, slipped there as is his way, to rest upon me like a mark of tenderness that will not dissolve or shift with time. But you left me, I tell him, pressing my face inside the channels of his throat to breathe the sweetness of his skin. How could you do such a thing? Even after what I did, still, how could you leave me, throw away my life like that, deliberately?

My face is rivered in tears to think of how he left me with nothing but the memory of him to torment me and drive me blackened from myself with missing him. How could you have thought I'd be able to stay alive, I ask him, with only a shell of myself to remember you by, with only unanswered echoes of a life split in two by your departure? Because I was left with love of what? Of you, or of your memory? You killed the self I loved. And how could you have taken that life from me?

I am inside the shelter of his arms, feeling the inevitability of death without emotion, the movement forwards to this ending without remorse now at my side since it's nothing more than logic that's shifting me so fast along, my days hurried to their conclusion with no more passion and anguish than a mathematical sum.

Still I have his voice against my ear, though steadier now and quiet. No, no, you must not think this is the way your life must go. Don't you see that you are all that's left of us, so you must live and for as long as possible, draw out the lovely skein of ourselves, remembering everything and honouring life that way with your own. Do you see? The thread must not be broken.

But the sea is ready, impatient for me to slip inside, and his voice is becoming insubstantial, faint and unbelievable among the flush of air across water speeding there to hurry me to jump. And anyway you are wrong, my love – his words like silver hooks to draw me back to life – that's not how I died at all. It didn't happen like that. And how could you imagine such a thing?

I have the weight raised off my right foot, ready to step into the sea. His voice, so quiet, is audible by one tone above the meagre static of the ruffled water. When I stop my breath I can hear him clearly, as though I'd tuned in to a distant radio station transmitting across a peaceful desert. His voice is dignified, insistent. No, that's not at all how that day happened. And as he speaks, the boat seems to be suspended beyond all motion, floating more in time than space.

Listen, he says to me, this is how it was: I'm standing here looking over the edge and laughing, actually, at the reflection of myself, almost perfectly mirrored back at me in the glassy sea. I'm laughing as

I look at my reflection, because for the first time since our son's death, I've caught myself smiling, suddenly able to see an end to all our grieving after him – just the way you turned so fast to me last night and held me as you used to do until the morning, fierce against you and full of needfulness that I swear I thought you'd never feel for me again, as though your sadness had tripped that switch of love forever in your heart, leaving me alone – but there you are, entwined about me, and showing me so plainly and with such faith that we can sneak back along the exact same track that we were ever fixed upon, loving one another just as we did when we were young, and I'm overfull of love for you at this moment of sitting out there in this boat, as sore as ever now with missing you.

So here I am grinning away like I'm soft in the head, I suppose, laughing at the lonely sight of myself so long a torment, now only a statement of intent: I have to get back to you, complete the picture of you and me, the one beside the other as we've always been and always ought to be. And I'm feeling not one slightest shred of the driven fear that always, until that moment, is waiting in the sea to taunt me, draw me back there every day to see what I can do to be free of it, though I'm always failing as it's forever ready there to catch me out if only I am weak enough to let it – until this moment, when it's as though I'm blessed with a bolt of perfect clarity, a heaven-cast gift of revelation like our shooting star, fast across the sky, of all possible explanations of what goes on between two people, and gone before anyone else alive has even caught a wink of it.

Listening to his voice, my heartbeat is loud and high inside my chest so that my throat is tight with nerves of expectation. A gull goes silent overhead to join a flock far distant in the east, and every second, so it seems, the sky is growing brighter, more reflective of the dancing blue beneath. His lips are close against my ear, each word a secret gift as he continues.

I see in a flash how wrong I am to be defeated by the darkness, since it's only the thing that makes the light burn brightly, and can it be so simple, this sure truth? So I'm setting my back to all the menaces of the sea and fixing my eyes instead upon the land, remembering the great long years of nightfall when you'd go upstairs with our sweet son just after dusk had deepened into evening, and you'd set a lamp there burning in the attic room, confident that I'd see it from out at sea and that way come more quickly home, guided back towards you both. Even now I have the expression on your face exactly there to recollection as you told me the way you'd do this every night without fail, how it was a little ritual between the two of you when I was late in coming home.

Momentarily he pauses, his eyes turned inwards as he thinks upon this vision. You both set that light there burning, even though you knew I'd be incapable of seeing it if I was in danger, or lost. But that by the time I was safely back in harbour I'd see that you had kept the faith I would return, and that that would be enough. Yet in truth there were a hundred lights and no way of knowing which one was yours. They'd be gleaming on the water as I came round the headland in sight of the village, and the moment I glimpsed home I'd shut my eyes and that way, in great secrecy, I would see your light in vivid separation from the others and be calm.

He smiles at me as he says this, and I do not breathe, so needful am I of his words, as though with every syllable I'm being hitched back up to life, the speed beneath me almost tangible. *Go on*, I whisper, and the quickening breeze scatters my words, dissolves them into air. His voice is light and almost playful.

Suddenly I realise that the fish can go scot-free today, for I'll not chase them – he's laughing as he continues with his tale. So I stow my nets away, back in the bows, and decide I'll turn instead for home, so I can be with you, close along beside you as I ought to, *have* to be, my love, and so I am and always will be. So I'm tussling with the nets, setting them straight and out of the way, when my foot catches beneath the bag you brought my lunch in, do you remember how you rushed to give it to me in the street? So my foot catches there and I'm kicking myself free of it as I start the engine up again, the breeze tickling my face and making me laugh still harder as I turn about to head for home, when suddenly I slip, like this –

He demonstrates, his arms catching at nothing but air, slipping fast as warm silk through my fingers, his smile vanishing as he realises, too late, that he has lost his footing and is shot straight overboard, sunk instantly below the flat calm of the sea, the weight of stones bearing him fast beneath, with nothing any living soul could ever possibly have done to steady up his sleek descent right to the centre of the ocean, finding out the other life that's there amongst the buzzing multitude of tides. And so the sea swallows him with one wide opening of its throat – despite whatever protests and defiance then were thrashing in his heart – it swallows him whole, and shuts its blind black eye to what's been done.

A fine mist has turned the surface of the water pale beneath a light that's paler still: morning is only a few hours old, and the sun gleams flat and low against a sky with no intensity or depth of colour – just a gradual brightening that bestows wakefulness on everything, as though light was life, and no vividness were possible without it. There is no heat yet in the daylight, and the air is sharp. I fill my lungs with it, and swear I can sense the season's change there, as the year begins its tilt towards the start of autumn.

When I look over the side of the boat, I can see the faintest writhe of green: forests of kelp have been disturbed by last night's storm, and it's as though the land itself was upset by the frenzy out at sea, mimicking that turmoil with a mirror-vision many miles beneath.

But the boat is steady now, and each second seems to sit more easily among the waves that do not break or even bear a single crest upon them, at least that I can see, but curve rotund about themselves like contained smoke, eddying within a dark green bottle. Colours swell and strengthen inside the glassiness. As the sun lifts higher, sand motes are caught like silk-winged moths in angled tunnels of light. The flickering tip of weed is malachite where the sun catches it.

The day is so close about me now. I can't ignore its readiness and peace. Each second seems recumbent in the one that flows before, as though time is unveiling an order to this scene of endless variation that can only be admired – not held, and not anticipated, so then not feared.

I have the moments growing calm and strong within me, as I look out on the day, and I feel no anguish, only the scars of anguish, which I am proud to bear. The sea is a solemn beast this morning, intent on going nowhere, happy merely to sit and have me stroke its recent-angered back – just like this, with the regular and soft comb of my keel.

But there is nothing upon the water, no sign or evidence of my love at all. The only sound is the steady bubble and rush beneath the keel, a sound without hidden meaning, just a noise that the ocean makes when it has a boat upon it, a sound like laughter but in fact nothing more than water running beneath wood and steel and finding pockets of air there and that way making noise. There's no mystery here that I can put a name to. There is only silence beneath everything: silence and memory. It is the double-edged trick of my imagination that has made me think of him and that way conjure him once more into a dream that I can live by. Because look, it is entirely true, I am alive when I had planned to die. Then love's the difference between life and death? Here's a proof that that is so: I am still alive.

My heart is beating steady as I aim the boat once more for shore. I can see so little of the land but it's enough. The faint green of it is shining in the early light of dawn, leading me back towards the opening day. And there's a lifting motion of the water, pressing soft against the boat to keep it turned and willing in the flow of onshore tide. I'll find home eventually. He's in my heart to guide me, as near and precious as he ever was, my only way, unchanged, beloved.

The sea is lustrous, absolutely banished now of

trouble, spread wide open beneath the fine light from the sun so that it is golden as ripe cornfields caught at dawn. My face is warmed already by its early brightness, reminding me of a day so many years ago but handed to me like a gift that bears no debt with it at all – just the delight of memory, unburdened of the anguish that for so long has blackened it, so that I could see nothing without the darkness that surrounded it. And at last I'm free, I know this absolutely now, and free with the most valuable freedom that there is, my mind unfettered by the night that's held it, so that I could see no joy without the price I paid in losing it, could feel no pleasure without the bitterness of that pleasure's end.

It was the very last part of the summer, around midday, with the sun enormous in the sky so that we'd all been singed by the hours spent walking about in it, the two of us without hats as I remember, although our son had on a little yellow hat made out of straw – yes, this is how it happened. There was a gulping kind of breeze skipping off the sea and funnelled up to where we were, a mile or so out of the village, walking through the lanes to look for brambles – we'd found a few and munched them straight down, our fingers stained purplish and delicious. There'd been no harvest yet, though it would be soon, and the fields were heavy with swollen heads of corn making a golden sea out of the entire length of cliffs so that our son was yahooing his way down the pathway that cut between.

We were walking along a little behind him – and this is what made me think of it – the breeze flipped off his straw hat so with a yelp he leapt straight into the cornfield, running after it as it bounced along the surface of the corn as though upon a tilting stretch of water. With a sudden dive, I remember how he leapt to fall upon his hat to catch it and then lay hidden there, with just his skinny arm waving that hat at us – and then he disappeared from view.

So we stood there looking at the empty-seeming field that was alive then with his laughter: he was shimmying his way towards us on his belly and we weren't supposed to know he was there. But we could hear his giggles – Coming to get you! – until he leapt out, pretending to be an angry fish, or so he said, Fresh out of Davy Jones's locker come to get you, he laughed, his knees covered in soil dust, corn husks stuck in his hair, making him all rascally when he pretended to fight as his dad hoisted him onto his shoulders with great growls, the three of us tearing off down the hillside, and later, back into the village, exhausted by heat and a day of perfect happiness, which now, for the first time in years, I can see again exactly as it happened, brightly and true, without the covering darkness of despair but exactly as it was, one day amongst so many others similarly lit with joy.

In fact, thinking on it now, I half imagine that it is an impression multiplied, perhaps, by many other likewise lovely days of summer – we would so often go to walk along the clifftops before harvest – and I remember our son's joke about chewing cornheads to make bread inside his belly, and once I even caught him mashing grain with a stone he'd smuggled into his bedroom. Look! – he'd been triumphant – I've discovered flour!

I'm smiling to myself as I remember this, almost able to hear again his boyish giggles beneath the golden flux of corn, golden as the sea itself this moment as the sun goes inching ever higher from the dark horizon. So here I am looking out at the water with no boat but mine upon it. Is that true? I wonder, turning right round to see if there's anyone else but me here, and the memory of my love. And in fact over in the north-east there's a faint smudge of boat-shaped stuff and my heart jumps, though only slightly, as I notice it. Damn fool coming out to here to find him, I curse myself, though smiling at my foolishness, When all along he was in your heart and never moving from that place.

The boat is soft beneath me, the wood of the hull washed smooth to the touch. The paintwork gleams where daylight falls upon it, and it seems impossible that it's the same boat that withstood last night's storm – as though the first great wave should've shattered its frail shell as easy as break a Christmas bauble made of glass. With the engine off, there are few sounds, and I leave no trace upon the water, my eyes the only witness to say that I've been here at all.

I stand up steady within the boat. Can it be possible that in just twenty-four hours I've earned my sea legs? I am smiling to myself as I think on this, remembering how it was later that same day, when we'd returned from our clifftop ramble, that my love told our son the trick for staying sure-footed on both land and sea.

By then the day had long since ended and the moon was new. The sky was a shroud that couldn't quench the life out from the stars, and arched from north to south the Milky Way was dazzling, vivid as a rainbow. We were upstairs, putting our son to bed, and he was laughing at the story that his father told, of how everyone thought that he was drunk the first time he came back from sea, the way he could not walk straight for days after, he was so dizzy, reeling all about the place.

And so the thing to do is this – he opened wide the curtains, letting in the night – find a fixed point, or piece of brightness, the horizon, or a star, and keep your eyes set there, and that way you'll be steady and again yourself. It's hard to do, he whispered, reaching out to draw me close, and most likely you'll misplace which star is yours, or when there's rough weather, and sea and sky are all whisked up as one, maybe you'll lose sight of everything you know but that won't matter if you've understood the trick – to keep searching at whatever cost, as it's the search itself that'll keep you steady, set to true.

My love reflected lamplight in his eyes, and outside the waves were feathers on the shore, as kind as sleep.

I see the whole scene now, immaculate.

Sitting back down at the tiller, I have the hum of the sea beneath my feet, enjoying the fast shapes it makes along the slender bentwood hull. I tip my head back and let the sea air dance across my face and it feels fine, wonderful with land scents, the inquisitive twist of earth and smoke. I pause for a second, just before I start the engine, noticing how the boat seems to be held here, almost motionless, as though seized in the circle of the tide's embrace, or as though time itself has gathered all its strength into one day, enough by far to show the turning, rolling shape of things, which now roll on, the small boat's prow cutting fast and easy through the waves – and where they break, the water catching light.